KWAIDAN

KWAIDAN

Weird Tales From Japan

Lafcadio Hearn

ISBN 978-1-84068-302-8

Edited by Jack Hunter, Aaron Williamson

Cover: Hokusai, *Ghost Of Kohada Koheji* (1830)

Illustrations: Yoshitoshi, *36 Ghosts* (1889)

Introduction copyright © Jack Hunter 2011

Published 2012 by Shinbaku Books

© Creation Publishing 2012

III : From "Shadowings" (1900):

IV: From "Japanese Fairy-Tales" (1898):

INTRODUCTION

I : MYTHS AND LEGENDS OF JAPAN

The *Jigoku-zoshi* ("Hell Scrolls") from the 12th century are amongst the earliest, and bloodiest, accounts of human carnage in illustrated Japanese myth. Victims are burned, drowned in blood, crushed by fiery rocks, flayed, eaten alive by beasts, and have their bones pulverised by vicious, club-wielding *oni* (horned, clawed, fanged demons who may have multiple eyes and blue or red skin). This is the Buddhist concept of purgatory, where sinners have eight "great hells" and sixteen "lesser hells" to contend with.

Creatures in Hell (*Jigokudo*) are the lowliest and most degraded beings in the Buddhist *rokudo* ("six states of transmigration"), wracked by torture and characterized by aggression. Their gruesome torments were also depicted in such documents as the *Hekija-e* ("Exorcism Scrolls") and the *Jigokuhen Gobyobu* ("Hell Transformation Screens"), which were used in year-end repentance ceremonies, held at the Imperial Palace up until the Heian period, in which the names of the Buddhas were recited.

The creatures who inhabit the next level of existence are *gaki* – literally, "hungry ghosts", damned souls doomed to walk the earth in a state of eternal craving and starvation. They are shown in the *Gaki-zoshi* ("Hungry ghost scrolls") of the same period, scavenging in graveyards for scraps of corpse-meat and other human detritus. Invisible to the mortal eye, they are skeletal with distended bellies, diseased, and repugnant. Their existence helped to account for natural processes such as bacterial decay that the medieval Japanese perceived, but were unable to explain in a scientific way.

Later illustrated scrolls include the *Bussetsu-jûôkyô* ("Sutra of the Ten Kings of Hell", 1594), in which the ten infernal monarchs – Shinkou, Shokou, Soutei, Gokan, Enma, Henjyou, Taizan, Byoudou, Toshi, and Gotoutenrin – were documented in glorious detail.

Although *oni*, the guardians of Hell, are perhaps the most fearsome of all creatures in Japanese demonology, there are a host of other equally bizarre beings in their supernatural spectrum, classified under the general name of *yokai* (literally, "a bewitching apparition"). In the Edo period, when *ukiyo-e* (mass-produced woodblock prints) began to flourish, numerous artistic works sought to document them. One of the most notable of these was the *Hyakkai Zukkan*, a collection of picture scrolls completed in 1737 by Sawaki Suushi. Suushi's garish pantheon of grotesqueries would serve as an inspiration to countless other artists. Among the creatures he documented are: *ushi-oni* ("cow devil"), a sea-monster with the head of a bull and the body of a giant spider or crab; *nure-onna* ("wet woman"), an amphibious vampire with the head of a human female and the body of a gigantic snake; *ouni*, a mountain hag with a huge mouth and thick, black hair covering her entire body; and *inugami*, a dog-demon.

Another *yokai* scroll of the same century was the *Ooishi Hyoroku Monogatari*, illustrating the story of a young warrior and his encounters with *kitsune* (shape-shifting foxes) who turn into various demonic forms. In the 1770s, the scholar and artist Toriyama Sekien began the enormous undertaking of compiling an exhaustive compendium of every known type of *obake* or *bakemono* – two terms which refer to any kind of supernatural being, including demons, monsters and ghosts. 1781 saw the very first edition of the legendary *Gazu Hyakki Yako* – "The Hundred Demons' Night Parade". Some of the most notable *obake* in this scroll and its subsequent variations (collectively known as *Hyakki Yagyu Emaki*) included the *rokurokubi*, a vampiric female demon with a long extendable neck, the *bakeneko* or *nekomata*, a monster cat, and *yuki-onna*, a snow-woman who can freeze men to death. It should be noted that Toriyama added some creatures of his own invention that did not originate in Japanese folklore.

The popularization and commercialization of *yokai* continued into the 19th century, exemplified by the creation of *obake karuta* playing cards, and many of the greatest *ukiyo-e* artists, including Yoshitoshi – whose art is featured in this new edition of **Kwaidan** - Hokusai, Kunisada, Kuniyoshi, Yoshitsuya and Kyosai, created works with supernatural themes in which their imaginations were unleashed to produce often dazzling, sometimes disturbing designs.

One of the most popular heroes in Japanese

legend was Minamoto no Yorimitsu (948-1021, also known as Raiko, a demon-slayer and exorcist. Assisted by his loyal servant Sakata Kintoki (also known as Kintaro or Golden Boy), Raiko's chief adversary was the *Tsuchigumo*, or Ground Spider, a monstrous giant arachnid who drank the blood of men and could also summon demons. Raiko encountered the spider whilst investigating a flying skull. Usually depicted in its eight-legged form, the Ground Spider would sometimes appear as a spider-woman in order to seduce its victims.

Japan also had many myths of the ocean, in particular the legend of Tamatori, the pearl-diver who stole a jewel from the Dragon-King of the sea. The fetishization of pearl-diving girls resulted in many *shunga* ("erotic prints") on the subject, and this tradition continued well into the 20th century when topless pearl-divers would feature in some of the very first Japanese sexploitation movies of the 1950s (including *Onna Shinjuo No Fukushu* ["Revenge Of The Pearl Queen"] and *Ama No Bakemono Yashiki* ["Haunted House Of Ama"]). Strange sea-creatures included water-dragons, giant fish, and fish-human hybrids such as the *samebito* (shark-man).

Other mythic creatures in Japanese folklore include the *tengu* (a ferocious mountain spirit with a bird's head or beak), the *nue* (a hybrid with the head of a monkey, the body of a raccoon dog, the legs of a tiger, and a snake as a tail), the *kappa* (a mutant frog water imp that feeds on humans) – and the king of them all, the dragon. *Ukiyo-e* also proliferates with images of grotesquely enlarged beasts of the more earthly variety, made weird by their exaggerated size. Giant snakes, lizards, centipedes, toads and other verminous creatures are conjured by curses and sent to plague the people of Japan, who must call on their valiant heroes to defend them. These behemoths are the precursors of *Godzilla* and other cinematic monsters of the 1950s who emerged in response to the advent of the Atomic Age.

Ghosts (*yurei*) have always played a prominent part in Japanese folklore. Although the majority of ghosts are female – due to the perceived strong passions of women – there are also some notable male ghosts. Male ghosts tend to fall into one of two categories – either a warrior who was killed in battle and cannot pull himself away from the historical events in which he figured (these appear mostly in Noh theatre), or an *onryo* (a vengeful ghost who returns from purgatory to avenge the wrongs done to them in life). *Funayurei* – the ghosts of those who perish at sea – are also nearly always of the male variety. Famous examples of male ghosts include the peasant leader Sakura Sogoro, the painter Kohada Koheiji, and drowned Taira general Tomomori.

The female ghost is perhaps the most recognizable figure in Japanese horror culture, and appears in several differing types; the cat-ghost vampire, the seductress ghost who initiates a post-death love affair with a living human, the *ubume* or mother ghost who died leaving her children behind and returns to care for them, the *yuki-onna* or snow-lady, the lethal *yurei* who suffered badly in life or was murdered by their lover, and whose powerful emotions of jealousy, sorrow, or rage at the moment of death brings them to seek terrible revenge. This last phantom is the one made known globally at the turn of the 20th century through the success of Japanese ghost films such as *Ringu* ("The Ring") and *Ju-On* ("The Grudge"). Their traditional appearance – long black hair in disarray over the face, white skin and white burial clothing – goes back to the very first *ukiyo-e* images of such creatures, of which the original is said to be Maruyama Okyo's painting of the ghost of Oyuki, from1750. The only difference with these cinematic *yurei* and the *yurei* of *ukiyo-e* is that the latter generally have no lower limbs, symbolising their disconnection with corporeality. Finally, one of the strangest *yurei* is the *ikiryo*, or "living spirit" – the ghost of a person still alive. An *ikiryo* may detach itself from the body under the influence of intense rage, and proceed to haunt and torment the individual by whom the rage was caused. The opposite term, *shiryo*, is used when stressing the ghost of a dead person.

One of Japan's most famous *yurei* is Oiwa, who appears in *Yotsuya Kaidan* ("Ghost Story of Yotsuya"), a story written first as a play in 1825 and later adapted for *kabuki* theatre and a host of films. Oiwa, poisoned and disfigured by her treacherous husband Iemon, has been depicted by many *ukiyo-e* artists as her ghost emerges from a lantern to take violent revenge.

Another famous female ghost is Okiku, a maid who breaks one of the ten gilded plates that are the legacy of the treasure house of Aoyama, and is punished by death. Her vengeful spirit emerges night after night from the well where she was drowned, counting the plates in a hideous voice until Aoyama is driven to commit suicide.

Oyuki, Oiwa and Okiku were the prototypes for a slew of *yurei* in popular fiction and *ukiyo-e*, growing ever more gruesome in appearance as the 19th century progressed.

It was from this rich, often grotesque pool of myth and lore that the writer Lafcadio Hearn was able to draw the weird tales which make up his collected *kwaidan* or *kaidan* ("ghost stories").

II : LAFCADIO HEARN AND *KWAIDAN*

Lafcadio Hearn, born in 1850 of Irish-Greek descent, worked as a newspaper journalist in the USA during the 1870s, and achieved some renown for his lurid and sensationalistic style of reporting. He faced scandal when he married a black woman – which was then illegal and could result in charges of bestiality – and in 1877 obtained a divorce and relocated to New Orleans. After a decade in that city, he was sent to Japan with a commission as a newspaper correspondent. Hearn fell in love with the country, and stayed there to become a teacher. He married Koizumi Setsu, the daughter of a local *samurai* family, and became a naturalized Japanese, taking the name Koizumi Yakumo.

It was during the following years that Hearn produced numerous books about Japanese traditions and culture, of which *Kwaidan* (1903), a collection of exotic ghost stories, became the best known. His first books on Japan, however, were cultural studies such as *Glimpses of Unfamiliar Japan* (1894), *Out of the East: Reveries and Studies in New Japan* (1895), *Kokoro: Hints and Echoes of Japanese Inner Life* (1896), and *Gleanings in Buddha-Fields: Studies of Hand and Soul in the Far East* (1897). It was not until 1898 that he started to assemble volumes of traditional Japanese stories. These stories were drawn from ancient books of weird lore, such as *Shin-Chomon-Shu*, *Hyaku Monogatari*, *Uji-Jui-Monogatari-Sho*, *Otogi-Hyaku-Monogatari*, *Konséki-Monogatari*, and *Kibun-Anbai-yoshi*. Hearn pursued his writing until the very end; by 1904, he was a professor at Waseda University, but died of heart failure that same year, at the young age of 54.

This new Creation Oneiros edition of **Kwaidan** is unique among anthologies of Hearn's writings in that it draws the best weird tales from not only Hearn's original book of that name, but also his other, lesser-known collections: *Japanese Fairy-Tales* (1898), *Shadowings* (1900), and *Kottó* (1902). In all, the book includes twenty-nine stories, making it the most comprehensive selection currently available. The stories have been further enhanced with a selection of eighteen supernatural *ukiyo-e* images by master artist Yoshitoshi, giving a true taste of Japanese culture at its most bizarre and phantastic extremes.

KWAIDAN

WEIRD TALES FROM JAPAN

LAFCADIO HEARN

THE STORY OF MIMI-NASHI-HOICHI

More than seven hundred years ago, at Dan-no-ura, in the Straits of Shimonoseki, was fought the last battle of the long contest between the Heike, or Taira clan, and the Genji, or Minamoto clan. There the Heike perished utterly, with their women and children, and their infant emperor likewise – now remembered as Antoku Tenno. And that sea and shore have been haunted for seven hundred years... strange crabs are found there, called Heike crabs, which have human faces on their backs, and are said to be the spirits of the Heike warriors. But there are many strange things to be seen and heard along that coast. On dark nights thousands of ghostly fires hover about the beach, or flit above the waves – pale lights which the fishermen call *Oni-bi*, or demon-fires; and, whenever the winds are up, a sound of great shouting comes from that sea, like a clamour of battle.

In former years the Heike were much more restless than they now are. They would rise about ships passing in the night, and try to sink them; and at all times they would watch for swimmers, to pull them down. It was in order to appease those dead that the Buddhist temple, Amidaji, was built at Akamagaseki. A cemetery also was made close by, near the beach; and within it were set up monuments inscribed with the names of the drowned emperor and of his great vassals; and Buddhist services were regularly performed there, on behalf of the spirits of them. After the temple had been built, and the tombs erected, the Heike gave less trouble than before; but they continued to do queer things at intervals, proving that they had not found the perfect peace.

Some centuries ago there lived at Akamagaseki a blind man named Hoichi, who was famed for his skill in recitation and in playing upon the *biwa*[1]. From childhood he had been trained to recite and to play; and while yet a lad he had surpassed his teachers. As a professional *biwa-hoshi* he became famous chiefly by his recitations of the history of the Heike and the Genji; and it is said that when he sang the song of the battle of Dan-no-ura "even the goblins [*kijin*] could not refrain from tears".

At the outset of his career, Hoichi was very poor; but he found a good friend to help him. The priest of the Amidaji was fond of poetry and music; and he often invited Hoichi to the temple, to play and recite. Afterwards, being much impressed by the wonderful skill of the lad, the priest proposed that Hoichi should make the temple his home; and this offer was gratefully accepted. Hoichi was given a room in the temple-building; and, in return for food and lodging, he was required only to gratify the priest with a musical performance on certain evenings, when otherwise disengaged.

One summer night the priest was called away, to perform a Buddhist service at the house of a dead parishioner; and he went there with his acolyte, leaving Hoichi alone in the temple. It was a hot night; and the blind man sought to cool himself on the verandah before his sleeping-room. The verandah overlooked a small garden in the rear of the Amidaji. There Hoichi waited for the priest's return, and tried to relieve his solitude by practicing upon his *biwa*. Midnight passed; and the priest did not appear. But the atmosphere was still too warm for comfort within doors; and Hoichi remained outside. At last he heard steps approaching from the back gate. Somebody crossed the garden, advanced to the verandah, and halted directly in front of him – but it was not the priest. A deep voice called the blind man's name, abruptly and unceremoniously, in the manner of a *samurai* summoning an inferior:

"Hoichi!"

"*Hai!*" answered the blind man, frightened by the menace in the voice, "I am blind! – I cannot know who calls!"

"There is nothing to fear," the stranger exclaimed, speaking more gently. "I am stopping near this temple, and have been sent to you with a message. My present lord, a person of exceedingly high rank, is now staying in Akamagaseki, with many noble attendants. He wished to view the scene of the battle of Dan-no-ura; and today he visited that place. Having heard of your skill in reciting the story of the battle, he now desires to hear your performance: so you will take your *biwa* and come with me at once to the house where the august assembly is waiting."

In those times, the order of a *samurai* was not to be lightly disobeyed. Hoichi donned his sandals, took his *biwa*, and went away with the stranger, who guided him deftly, but obliged him to walk very fast. The hand that guided was iron; and the clank of the warrior's stride proved him fully armed, probably some palace-guard on duty. Hoichi's first alarm was over: he began to imagine himself in good luck; for, remembering the retainer's assurance about a "person of exceedingly high rank," he thought that the lord who wished to hear the recitation could not be less than a daimyo of the first class. Presently the *samurai* halted; and Hoichi became aware that they had arrived at a large gateway; and he wondered, for he could not remember any large gate in that part of the town, except the main gate of the Amidaji. "*Kaimon!*" the *samurai* called to the guards, and there was a sound of unbarring; and the twain passed on. They traversed a space of garden, and halted again before some entrance; and the retainer cried in a loud voice, "Within there! I have brought Hoichi." Then came sounds of feet hurrying, and screens sliding, and rain-doors opening, and voices of women in converse. By the language of the women Hoichi knew them to be domestics in some noble household; but he could not imagine to what place he had been conducted. Little time was allowed him for conjecture. After he had been helped to mount several stone steps, upon the last of which he was told to leave his sandals, a woman's hand guided him along interminable reaches of polished planking, and round pillared angles too many to remember, and over widths amazing of matted floor, into the middle of some vast apartment. There he thought that many great people were assembled: the sound of the rustling of silk was like the sound of leaves in a forest. He heard also a great humming of voices, talking in undertones; and the speech was the speech of courts.

Hoichi was told to put himself at ease, and he found a kneeling-cushion ready for him. After having taken his place upon it, and tuned his instrument, the voice of a woman – whom he divined to be the *rojo*, or matron in charge of the female service – addressed him, saying,

"It is now required that the history of the Heike be recited, to the accompaniment of the *biwa*."

Now the entire recital would have required a time of many nights: therefore Hoichi ventured a question:

"As the whole of the story is not soon told, what portion is it augustly desired that I now recite?"

The woman's voice made answer:

"Recite the story of the battle at Dan-no-ura, for the pity of it is the most deep."

Then Hoichi lifted up his voice, and chanted the chant of the fight on the bitter sea, wonderfully making his *biwa* to sound like the straining of oars and the rushing of ships, the whirr and the hissing of arrows, the shouting and trampling of men, the crashing of steel upon helmets, the plunging of slain in the flood. And to left and right of him, in the pauses of his playing, he could hear voices murmuring praise: "How marvelous an artist!" – "Never in our own province was playing heard like this!" – "Not in all the empire is there another singer like Hoichi!" Then fresh courage came to him, and he played and sang yet better than before; and a hush of wonder deepened about him. But when at last he came to tell the fate of the fair and helpless, the piteous perishing of the women and children, and the death-leap of Nii-no-Ama, with the imperial infant in her arms, then all the listeners uttered together one long, long shuddering cry of anguish; and thereafter they wept and wailed so loudly and so wildly that the blind man was frightened by the violence and grief that he had made. For much time the sobbing and the wailing continued. But gradually the sounds of lamentation died away; and again, in the great stillness that followed, Hoichi heard the voice of the woman whom he supposed to be the *rojo*.

She said:

"Although we had been assured that you were a very skillful player upon the *biwa*, and without an equal in recitative, we did not know that any one could be so skillful as you have proved yourself tonight. Our lord has been pleased to say that he intends to bestow upon you a fitting reward. But he desires that you shall perform before him once every night for the next six nights – after which time he will probably make his august return-journey. tomorrow night, therefore, you are to come here at the same hour. The retainer who tonight conducted you will be sent for you... There is another matter about which I have been ordered to inform you. It is required that you shall speak to no one of your visits here, during the time of our lord's august sojourn at Akamagaseki. As he is traveling incognito, he commands that no mention of these things be made... You are now free to go back to your temple."

After Hoichi had duly expressed his thanks, a woman's hand conducted him to the entrance of the house, where the same retainer, who had before guided him, was waiting to take him home. The retainer led him to the verandah at the rear of the temple, and there bade him farewell.

It was almost dawn when Hoichi returned; but his absence from the temple had not been observed, as the priest, coming back at a very late hour, had supposed him asleep. During the day Hoichi was able to take some rest; and he said nothing about his strange adventure. In the middle of the following night the *samurai* again came for him, and led him to the august assembly, where he gave another recitation with the same success that had attended his previous performance. But during this second visit his absence from the temple was accidentally discovered; and after his return in the morning he was summoned to the presence of the priest, who said to him, in a tone of kindly reproach:

"We have been very anxious about you, friend Hoichi. To go out, blind and alone, at so late an hour, is dangerous. Why did you go without telling us? I could have ordered a servant to accompany you. And where have you been?"

Hoichi answered, evasively,

"Pardon me kind friend! I had to attend to some

private business; and I could not arrange the matter at any other hour."

The priest was surprised, rather than pained, by Hoichi's reticence: he felt it to be unnatural, and suspected something wrong. He feared that the blind lad had been bewitched or deluded by some evil spirits. He did not ask any more questions; but he privately instructed the men-servants of the temple to keep watch upon Hoichi's movements, and to follow him in case that he should again leave the temple after dark.

On the very next night, Hoichi was seen to leave the temple; and the servants immediately lighted their lanterns, and followed after him. But it was a rainy night, and very dark; and before the temple-folks could get to the roadway, Hoichi had disappeared. Evidently he had walked very fast – a strange thing, considering his blindness; for the road was in a bad condition. The men hurried through the streets, making inquiries at every house which Hoichi was accustomed to visit; but nobody could give them any news of him. At last, as they were returning to the temple by way of the shore, they were startled by the sound of a *biwa*, furiously played, in the cemetery of the Amidaji. Except for some ghostly fires – such as usually flitted there on dark nights – all was blackness in that direction. But the men at once hastened to the cemetery; and there, by the help of their lanterns, they discovered Hoichi, sitting alone in the rain before the memorial tomb of Antoku Tenno, making his *biwa* resound, and loudly chanting the chant of the battle of Dan-no-ura. And behind him, and about him, and everywhere above the tombs, the fires of the dead were burning, like candles. Never before had so great a host of *Oni-bi* appeared in the sight of mortal man...

"Hoichi San! Hoichi San!" the servants cried, "you are bewitched!... Hoichi San!"

But the blind man did not seem to hear. Strenuously he made his *biwa* to rattle and ring and clang; more and more wildly he chanted the chant of the battle of Dan-no-ura. They caught hold of him; they shouted into his ear,

"Hoichi San! Hoichi San! Come home with us at once!"

Reprovingly he spoke to them:

"To interrupt me in such a manner, before this august assembly, will not be tolerated."

Whereat, in spite of the weirdness of the thing, the servants could not help laughing. Sure that he had been bewitched, they now seized him, and pulled him up on his feet, and by main force hurried him back to the temple, where he was immediately relieved of his wet clothes, by order of the priest. Then the priest insisted upon a full explanation of his friend's astonishing behaviour.

Hoichi long hesitated to speak. But at last, finding that his conduct had really alarmed and angered the good priest, he decided to abandon his reserve; and he related everything that had happened from the time of first visit of the *samurai*.

The priest said:

"Hoichi, my poor friend, you are now in great

danger! How unfortunate that you did not tell me all this before! Your wonderful skill in music has indeed brought you into strange trouble. By this time you must be aware that you have not been visiting any house whatever, but have been passing your nights in the cemetery, among the tombs of the Heike; and it was before the memorial-tomb of Antoku Tenno that our people tonight found you, sitting in the rain. All that you have been imagining was illusion – except the calling of the dead. By once obeying them, you have put yourself in their power. If you obey them again, after what has already occurred, they will tear you in pieces. But they would have destroyed you, sooner or later, in any event... Now I shall not be able to remain with you tonight: I am called away to perform another service. But, before I go, it will be necessary to protect your body by writing holy texts upon it."

Before sundown the priest and his acolyte stripped Hoichi: then, with their writing-brushes, they traced upon his breast and back, head and face and neck, limbs and hands and feet, even upon the soles of his feet, and upon all parts of his body, the text of the holy sutra called *Hannya-Shin-Kyo*.[2] When this had been done, the priest instructed Hoichi, saying:

"tonight, as soon as I go away, you must seat yourself on the verandah, and wait. You will be called. But, whatever may happen, do not answer, and do not move. Say nothing and sit still – as if meditating. If you stir, or make any noise, you will be torn asunder. Do not get frightened; and do not think of calling for help – because no help could save you. If you do exactly as I tell you, the danger will pass, and you will have nothing more to fear."

After dark the priest and the acolyte went away; and Hoichi seated himself on the verandah, according to the instructions given him. He laid his *biwa* on the planking beside him, and, assuming the attitude of meditation, remained quite still, taking care not to cough, or to breathe audibly. For hours he stayed thus.

Then, from the roadway, he heard the steps coming. They passed the gate, crossed the garden, approached the verandah, stopped – directly in front of him.

"Hoichi!" the deep voice called. But the blind man held his breath, and sat motionless.

"Hoichi!" grimly called the voice a second time. Then a third time – savagely:

"Hoichi!"

Hoichi remained as still as a stone, and the voice grumbled:

"No answer! That won't do!... Must see where the fellow is..."

There was a noise of heavy feet mounting upon the verandah. The feet approached deliberately, halted beside him. Then, for long minutes, during which Hoichi felt his whole body shake to the beating of his heart, there was dead silence.

At last the gruff voice muttered close to him:

"Here is the *biwa*; but of the *biwa*-player I see only two ears!... So that explains why he did not answer: he had no mouth to answer with – there is nothing left of him but his ears... Now to my lord those ears I will take – in proof that the august commands have been obeyed, so far as was possible..."

At that instant Hoichi felt his ears gripped by fingers of iron, and torn off! Great as the pain was, he gave no cry. The heavy footfalls receded along the verandah, descended into the garden, passed out to the roadway, ceased. From either side of his head, the blind man felt a thick warm trickling; but he dared not lift his hands...

Before sunrise the priest came back. He hastened at once to the verandah in the rear, stepped and slipped upon something clammy, and uttered a cry of horror; for he say, by the light of his lantern, that the clamminess was blood. But he perceived Hoichi sitting there, in the attitude of meditation, with the blood still oozing from his wounds.

"My poor Hoichi!" cried the startled priest, "what is this?... You have been hurt?"

At the sound of his friend's voice, the blind man felt safe. He burst out sobbing, and tearfully told his adventure of the night.

"Poor, poor Hoichi!" the priest exclaimed; "all my fault! – my very grievous fault!... Everywhere upon your body the holy texts had been written – except upon your ears! I trusted my acolyte to do that part of the work; and it was very, very wrong of me not to have made sure that he had done it!... Well, the matter cannot now be helped; we can only try to heal your hurts as soon as possible... Cheer up, friend! The danger is now well over.

You will never again be troubled by those visitors."

With the aid of a good doctor, Hoichi soon recovered from his injuries. The story of his strange adventure spread far and wide, and soon made him famous. Many noble persons went to Akamagaseki to hear him recite; and large presents of money were given to him, so that he became a wealthy man... But from the time of his adventure, he was known only by the appellation of *Mimi-nashi-Hoichi*: "Hoichi-the-Earless."

NOTES

1. The *biwa*, a kind of four-stringed lute, is chiefly used in musical recitative. Formerly the professional minstrels who recited the *Heike-Monogatari*, and other tragical histories, were called *biwa-hoshi*, or "lute-priests". The origin of this appellation is not clear; but it is possible that it may have been suggested by the fact that "lute-priests" as well as blind shampooers, had their heads shaven, like Buddhist priests. The *biwa* is played with a kind of plectrum, called *bachi*, usually made of horn.

2. The smaller Pragna-Paramita-Hridaya-Sutra is thus called in Japanese. Both the smaller and larger sutras called Pragna-Paramita ("Transcendent Wisdom") have been translated by the late Professor Max Muller, and can be found in volume xlix. of the *Sacred Books of the East* ("Buddhist Mahayana Sutras"). Apropos of the magical use of the text, as described in this story, it is worth remarking that the subject of the sutra is the Doctrine of the Emptiness of Forms, that is to say, of the unreal character of all phenomena or noumena... "Form is emptiness; and emptiness is form. Emptiness is not different from form; form is not different from emptiness. What is form – that is emptiness. What is emptiness – that is form... Perception, name, concept, and knowledge, are also emptiness... There is no eye, ear, nose, tongue, body, and mind... But when the envelopment of consciousness has been annihilated, then he [the seeker] becomes free from all fear, and beyond the reach of change, enjoying final Nirvana."

OSHIDORI

There was a falconer and hunter, named Sonjo, who lived in the district called Tamura-no-Go, of the province of Mutsu. One day he went out hunting, and could not find any game. But on his way home, at a place called Akanuma, he perceived a pair of *oshidori* (mandarin-ducks), swimming together in a river that he was about to cross. To kill *oshidori* is not good; but Sonjo happened to be very hungry, and he shot at the pair. His arrow pierced the male: the female escaped into the rushes of the further shore, and disappeared. Sonjo took the dead bird home, and cooked it.

That night he dreamed a dreary dream. It seemed to him that a beautiful woman came into his room, and stood by his pillow, and began to weep. So bitterly did she weep that Sonjo felt as if his heart were being torn out while he listened. And the woman cried to him: "Why, oh! why did you kill him? Of what wrong was he guilty?... At Akanuma we were so happy together, and you killed him!... What harm did he ever do you? Do you even know what you have done? Oh! do you know what a cruel, what a wicked thing you have done?... Me too you have killed, for I will not live without my husband!... Only to tell you this I came."... Then again she wept aloud, so bitterly that the voice of her crying pierced into the marrow of the listener's bones; and she sobbed out the words of this poem:

Hi kurureba
Sasoeshi mono wo –
Akanuma no
Makomo no kure no
Hitori-ne zo uki!

("At the coming of twilight I invited him to return with me! Now to sleep alone in the shadow of the rushes of Akanuma – ah! what misery unspeakable!")[1]

And after having uttered these verses she exclaimed: "Ah, you do not know – you cannot know what you have done! But tomorrow, when you go to Akanuma, you will see, you will see..." So saying, and weeping very piteously, she went away.

When Sonjo awoke in the morning, this dream remained so vivid in his mind that he was greatly troubled. He remembered the words: "But tomorrow, when you go to Akanuma, you will see, you will see." And he resolved to go there at once, that he might learn whether his dream was anything more than a dream.

So he went to Akanuma; and there, when he came to the river-bank, he saw the female *oshidori* swimming alone. In the same moment the bird perceived Sonjo; but, instead of trying to escape, she swam straight towards him, looking at him the while in a strange fixed way. Then, with her beak, she suddenly tore open her own body, and died before the hunter's eyes...

Sonjo shaved his head, and became a priest.

NOTES

1. There is a pathetic double meaning in the third verse; for the syllables composing the proper name *Akanuma* ("Red Marsh") may also be read as *akanu-ma*, signifying "the time of our inseparable (or delightful) relation." So the poem can also be thus rendered: "At the coming of twilight I invited him to return with me! Now, after the time of that happy relation, what misery for the one who must sleep alone in the shadow of the rushes!" (*The makomo* is a short of large rush, used for making baskets.)

THE STORY OF O-TEI

A long time ago, in the town of Niigata, in the province of Echizen, there lived a man called Nagao Chosei.

Nagao was the son of a physician, and was educated for his father's profession. At an early age he had been betrothed to a girl called O-Tei, the daughter of one of his father's friends; and both families had agreed that the wedding should take place as soon as Nagao had finished his studies. But the health of O-Tei proved to be weak; and in her fifteenth year she was attacked by a fatal consumption. When she became aware that she must die, she sent for Nagao to bid him farewell.

As he knelt at her bedside, she said to him:

"Nagao-Sama, my betrothed, we were promised to each other from the time of our childhood; and we were to have been married at the end of this year. But now I am going to die; the gods know what is best for us. If I were able to live for some years longer, I could only continue to be a cause of trouble and grief for others. With this frail body, I could not be a good wife; and therefore even to wish to live, for your sake, would be a very selfish wish. I am quite resigned to die; and I want you to promise that you will not grieve... Besides, I want to tell you that I think we shall meet again."...

"Indeed we shall meet again," Nagao answered earnestly. "And in that Pure Land there will be no pain of separation."

"Nay, nay!" she responded softly, "I meant not the Pure Land. I believe that we are destined to meet again in this world, although I shall be buried tomorrow."

Nagao looked at her wonderingly, and saw her smile at his wonder. She continued, in her gentle, dreamy voice,

"Yes, I mean in this world, in your own present life, Nagao-Sama... Providing, indeed, that you wish it. Only, for this thing to happen, I must again be born a girl, and grow up to womanhood. So you would have to wait. Fifteen – sixteen years: that is a long time... But, my promised husband, you are now only nineteen years old."...

Eager to soothe her dying moments, he answered tenderly:

"To wait for you, my betrothed, were no less a joy than a duty. We are pledged to each other for the time of seven existences."

"But you doubt?" she questioned, watching his face.

"My dear one," he answered, "I doubt whether I should be able to know you in another body, under another name, unless you can tell me of a sign or token."

"That I cannot do," she said. "Only the Gods and the Buddhas know how and where we shall meet. But I am sure – very, very sure – that, if you be not unwilling to receive me, I shall be able to come back to you... Remember these words of mine."...

She ceased to speak; and her eyes closed. She

was dead.

Nagao had been sincerely attached to O-Tei; and his grief was deep. He had a mortuary tablet made, inscribed with her *zokumyo*;[1] and he placed the tablet in his *butsudan* [household shrine] and every day set offerings before it. He thought a great deal about the strange things that O-Tei had said to him just before her death; and, in the hope of pleasing her spirit, he wrote a solemn promise to wed her if she could ever return to him in another body. This written promise he sealed with his seal, and placed in the *butsudan* beside the mortuary tablet of O-Tei.

Nevertheless, as Nagao was an only son, it was necessary that he should marry. He soon found himself obliged to yield to the wishes of his family, and to accept a wife of his father's choosing. After his marriage he continued to set offerings before the tablet of O-Tei; and he never failed to remember her with affection. But by degrees her image became dim in his memory, like a dream that is hard to recall. And the years went by.

During those years many misfortunes came upon him. He lost his parents by death, then his wife and his only child. So that he found himself alone in the world. He abandoned his desolate home, and set out upon a long journey in the hope of forgetting his sorrows.

One day, in the course of his travels, he arrived at Ikao, a mountain-village still famed for its thermal springs, and for the beautiful scenery of its neighbourhood. In the village-inn at which he stopped, a young girl came to wait upon him; and, at the first sight of her face, he felt his heart leap as it had never leaped before. So strangely did she resemble O-Tei that he pinched himself to make sure that he was not dreaming. As she went and came, bringing fire and food, or arranging the chamber of the guest, her every attitude and motion revived in him some gracious memory of the girl to whom he had been pledged in his youth. He spoke to her; and she responded in a soft, clear voice of which the sweetness saddened him with a sadness of other days.

Then, in great wonder, he questioned her, saying:

"Elder Sister, so much do you look like a person whom I knew long ago, that I was startled when you first entered this room. Pardon me, therefore, for asking what is your native place, and what is your name?"

Immediately, and in the unforgotten voice of the dead, she thus made answer:

"My name is O-Tei; and you are Nagao Chosei of Echigo, my promised husband. Seventeen years ago, I died in Niigata: then you made in writing a promise to marry me if ever I could come back to this world in the body of a woman; and you sealed that written promise with your seal, and put it in the *butsudan*, beside the tablet inscribed with my name. And therefore I came back..."

As she uttered these last words, she fell unconscious.

Nagao married her; and the marriage was a happy one. But at no time afterwards could she remember what she had told him in answer to his question at Ikao: neither could she remember anything of her previous existence. The recollection of the former birth, mysteriously kindled in the moment of that meeting, had again become obscured, and so thereafter remained.

NOTES

1. The Buddhist term *zokumyo* ("profane name") signifies the personal name, borne during life, in contradistinction to the *kaimyo* ("sila-name") or *homyo* ("law-name") given after death – religious posthumous appellations inscribed upon the tomb, and upon the mortuary tablet in the parish-temple.

UBAZAKURA

Three hundred years ago, in the village called Asamimura, in the district called Onsengori, in the province of Iyo, there lived a good man named Tokubei. This Tokubei was the richest person in the district, and the *muraosa*, or headman, of the village. In most matters he was fortunate; but he reached the age of forty without knowing the happiness of becoming a father. Therefore he and his wife, in the affliction of their childlessness, addressed many prayers to the divinity Fudo Myo O, who had a famous temple, called Saihoji, in Asamimura.

At last their prayers were heard: the wife of Tokubei gave birth to a daughter. The child was very pretty; and she received the name of Tsuyu. As the mother's milk was deficient, a milk-nurse, called O-Sode, was hired for the little one.

O-Tsuyu grew up to be a very beautiful girl; but at the age of fifteen she fell sick, and the doctors thought that she was going to die. In that time the nurse O-Sode, who loved O-Tsuyu with a real mother's love, went to the temple Saihoji, and fervently prayed to Fudo-Sama on behalf of the girl. Every day, for twenty-one days, she went to the temple and prayed; and at the end of that time, O-Tsuyu suddenly and completely recovered.

Then there was great rejoicing in the house of

Tokubei; and he gave a feast to all his friends in celebration of the happy event. But on the night of the feast the nurse O-Sode was suddenly taken ill; and on the following morning, the doctor, who had been summoned to attend her, announced that she was dying.

Then the family, in great sorrow, gathered about her bed, to bid her farewell. But she said to them:

"It is time that I should tell you something which you do not know. My prayer has been heard. I besought Fudo-Sama that I might be permitted to die in the place of O-Tsuyu; and this great favour has been granted me. Therefore you must not grieve about my death... But I have one request to make. I promised Fudo-Sama that I would have a cherry-tree planted in the garden of Saihoji, for a thank-offering and a commemoration. Now I shall not be able myself to plant the tree there: so I must beg that you will fulfill that vow for me... Good-bye, dear friends; and remember that I was happy to die for O-Tsuyu's sake."

After the funeral of O-Sode, a young cherry-tree, the finest that could be found, was planted in the garden of Saihoji by the parents of O-Tsuyu. The tree grew and flourished; and on the sixteenth day of the second month of the following year – the anniversary of O-Sode's death – it blossomed in a wonderful way. So it continued to blossom for two hundred and fifty-four years, always upon the sixteenth day of the second month; and its flowers, pink and white, were like the nipples of a woman's breasts, bedewed with milk. And the people called it *Ubazakura*, the Cherry-tree of the Milk-Nurse.

DIPLOMACY

It had been ordered that the execution should take place in the garden of the *yashiki*[1]. So the man was taken there, and made to kneel down in a wide sanded space crossed by a line of *tobi-ishi*, or stepping-stones, such as you may still see in Japanese landscape-gardens. His arms were bound behind him. Retainers brought water in buckets, and rice-bags filled with pebbles; and they packed the rice-bags round the kneeling man, so wedging him in that he could not move. The master came, and observed the arrangements. He found them satisfactory, and made no remarks.

Suddenly the condemned man cried out to him:

"Honuored Sir, the fault for which I have been doomed I did not wittingly commit. It was only my very great stupidity which caused the fault. Having been born stupid, by reason of my Karma, I could not always help making mistakes. But to kill a man for being stupid is wrong, and that wrong will be repaid. So surely as you kill me, so surely shall I be avenged; out of the resentment that you provoke will come the vengeance; and evil will be rendered for evil..."

If any person be killed while feeling strong resentment, the ghost of that person will be able to take vengeance upon the killer. This the *samurai* knew. He replied very gently, almost caressingly:

"We shall allow you to frighten us as much as you please – after you are dead. But it is difficult to believe that you mean what you say. Will you try to give us some sign of your great resentment – after your head has been cut off?"

"Assuredly I will," answered the man.

"Very well," said the *samurai*, drawing his long sword; "I am now going to cut off your head. Directly in front of you there is a stepping-stone. After your head has been cut off, try to bite the stepping-stone. If your angry ghost can help you to do that, some of us may be frightened... Will you try to bite the stone?"

"I will bite it!" cried the man, in great anger, "I will bite it! I will bite–"

There was a flash, a swish, a crunching thud: the bound body bowed over the rice sacks, two long blood-jets pumping from the shorn neck; and the head rolled upon the sand. Heavily toward the stepping-stone it rolled: then, suddenly bounding, it caught the upper edge of the stone between its teeth, clung desperately for a moment, and dropped inert.

None spoke; but the retainers stared in horror at their master. He seemed to be quite unconcerned. He merely held out his sword to the nearest attendant, who, with a wooden dipper, poured water over the blade from haft to point, and then carefully wiped the steel several times with sheets of soft paper... And thus ended the ceremonial part of the incident.

For months thereafter, the retainers and the domestics lived in ceaseless fear of ghostly visitation.

None of them doubted that the promised vengeance would come; and their constant terror caused them to hear and to see much that did not exist. They became afraid of the sound of the wind in the bamboos, afraid even of the stirring of shadows in the garden. At last, after taking counsel together, they decided to petition their master to have a *Segaki*-service[2] performed on behalf of the vengeful spirit.

"Quite unnecessary," the *samurai* said, when his chief retainer had uttered the general wish... "I understand that the desire of a dying man for revenge may be a cause for fear. But in this case there is nothing to fear."

The retainer looked at his master beseechingly, but hesitated to ask the reason of the alarming confidence.

"Oh, the reason is simple enough," declared the *samurai*, divining the unspoken doubt. "Only the very last intention of the fellow could have been dangerous; and when I challenged him to give me the sign, I diverted his mind from the desire of revenge. He died with the set purpose of biting the stepping-stone; and that purpose he was able to accomplish, but nothing else. All the rest he must have forgotten... So you need not feel any further anxiety about the matter."

And indeed, the dead man gave no more trouble.

NOTES

1. *Yashiki*: the spacious house and grounds of a wealthy person.

2. *Segaki*-service: Buddhist service for the dead, especially those supposed to have entered into the condition of *gaki*, or hungry ghosts.

OF A MIRROR AND A BELL

Eight centuries ago, the priests of Mugenyama, in the province of Totomi, wanted a big bell for their temple; and they asked the women of their parish to help them by contributing old bronze mirrors for bell-metal.

[Even today, in the courts of certain Japanese temples, you may see heaps of old bronze mirrors contributed for such a purpose. The largest collection of this kind that I ever saw was in the court of a temple of the Jodo sect, at Hakata, in Kyushu: the mirrors had been given for the making of a bronze statue of Amida, thirty-three feet high.]

There was at that time a young woman, a farmer's wife, living at Mugenyama, who presented her mirror to the temple, to be used for bell-metal. But afterwards she much regretted her mirror. She remembered things that her mother had told her about it; and she remembered that it had belonged, not only to her mother but to her mother's mother and grandmother; and she remembered some happy smiles which it had reflected. Of course, if she could have offered the priests a certain sum of money in place of the mirror, she could have asked them to give back her heirloom. But she had not the money necessary. Whenever she went to the temple, she saw her mirror lying in the court-yard, behind a railing, among hundreds of other mirrors heaped there together. She knew it by the *Sho-Chiku-Bai* in relief on the back of it – those three fortunate emblems of Pine, Bamboo, and Plumflower, which delighted her baby-eyes when her mother first showed her the mirror. She longed for some chance to steal the mirror, and hide it, that she might thereafter treasure it always. But the chance did not come; and she became very unhappy, felt as if she had foolishly given away a part of her life. She thought about the old saying that a mirror is the Soul of a Woman – a saying mystically expressed, by the Chinese character for Soul, upon the backs of many bronze mirrors – and she feared that it was true in weirder ways than she had before imagined. But she could not dare to speak of her pain to anybody.

Now, when all the mirrors contributed for the Mugenyama bell had been sent to the foundry, the bell-founders discovered that there was one mirror among them which would not melt. Again and again they tried to melt it; but it resisted all their efforts. Evidently the woman who had given that mirror to the temple must have regretted the giving. She had not presented her offering with all her heart; and therefore her selfish soul, remaining attached to the mirror, kept it hard and cold in the midst of the furnace.

Of course everybody heard of the matter, and everybody soon knew whose mirror it was that would not melt. And because of this public exposure of her secret fault, the poor woman became very much ashamed and very angry. And as she could not bear the shame, she drowned herself, after having written a farewell letter containing these words:

"*When I am dead, it will not be difficult to melt the mirror and to cast the bell. But, to the person who breaks that bell by ringing it, great wealth will be given by the ghost of me.*"

You must know that the last wish or promise of anybody who dies in anger, or performs suicide in anger, is generally supposed to possess a supernatural force. After the dead woman's mirror had been melted, and the bell had been successfully cast, people remembered the words of that letter. They felt sure that the spirit of the writer would give wealth to the breaker of the bell; and, as soon as the bell had been suspended in the court of the temple, they went in multitude to ring it. With all their might and main they swung the ringing-beam; but the bell proved to be a good bell, and it bravely withstood their assaults. Nevertheless, the people were not easily discouraged. Day after day, at all hours, they continued to ring the bell furiously, caring nothing whatever for the protests of the priests. So the ringing became an affliction; and the priests could not endure it; and they got rid of the bell by rolling it down the hill into a swamp. The swamp was deep, and swallowed it up – and that was the end of the bell. Only its legend remains; and in that legend it is called the *Mugen-Kane*, or Bell of Mugen.

Now there are queer old Japanese beliefs in the magical efficacy of a certain mental operation implied, though not described, by the verb *nazoraeru*. The word itself cannot be adequately rendered by any English word; for it is used in relation to many kinds of mimetic magic, as well as in relation to the performance of many religious acts of faith. Common meanings of *nazoraeru*, according to dictionaries, are "to imitate," "to compare," "to liken;" but the esoteric meaning is *to substitute, in imagination, one object or action for another, so as to bring about some magical or miraculous result.*

For example: you cannot afford to build a Buddhist temple; but you can easily lay a pebble before the image of the Buddha, with the same pious feeling that would prompt you to build a temple if you were rich enough to build one. The merit of so offering the pebble becomes equal, or almost equal, to the merit of erecting a temple... You cannot read the six thousand seven hundred and seventy-one volumes of the Buddhist texts; but you can make a revolving library, containing them, turn round, by pushing it like a windlass. And if you push with an earnest wish that you could read the six thousand seven hundred and seventy-one volumes, you will acquire the same merit has the reading of them would enable you to gain... So much will perhaps suffice to explain the religious meanings of *nazoraeru*.

The magical meanings could not all be explained without a great variety of examples; but, for present purposes, the following will serve. If you should make a little man of straw, for the same reason that Sister Helen made a little man of wax, and nail it, with nails not less than five inches long, to some tree in a temple-grove at the Hour of the Ox[1], and if the person, imaginatively represented by that little straw man, should die thereafter in atrocious agony, that would illustrate one signification of *nazoraeru*... Or, let us suppose that a robber has entered your house during the night, and carried away your valuables. If you can discover the footprints of that robber in your garden, and then promptly burn a very large *moxa* on each of them, the soles of the feet of the robber will become inflamed, and will allow him no rest until he returns, of his own accord, to put himself at your mercy. That is another kind of mimetic magic expressed by the term *nazoraeru*. And a third kind is illustrated by various legends of the *Mugen-Kane*.

After the bell had been rolled into the swamp, there was, of course, no more chance of ringing it in such wise as to break it. But persons who regretted this loss of opportunity would strike and break objects imaginatively substituted for the bell, thus hoping to please the spirit of the owner of the mirror that had made so much trouble. One of these persons was a woman called Umegae, famed in Japanese legend because of her relation to Kajiwara Kagesue, a warrior of the Heike clan. While the pair were traveling together, Kajiwara one day found himself in great straits for want of money; and Umegae, remembering the tradition of the Bell of Mugen, took a basin of bronze, and, mentally representing it to be the bell, beat upon it until she broke it, crying out, at the same time, for three hundred pieces of gold. A guest of the inn where the pair were stopping made inquiry as to the cause of the banging and the crying, and, on learning the story of the trouble, actually presented Umegae with three hundred *ryo* in gold. Afterwards a song was made about Umegae's basin of bronze; and that song is sung by dancing girls even to this day:

> *Umegae no chozubachi tataite*
> *O-kane ga deru naraba*
> *Mina San mi-uke wo*
> *Sore tanomimasu*

["If, by striking upon the wash-basin of Umegae, I could make honourable money come to me, then would I negotiate for the freedom of all my girl-comrades."]

After this happening, the fame of the *Mugen-Kane* became great; and many people followed the example of Umegae, thereby hoping to emulate her luck. Among these folk was a dissolute farmer who lived near Mugenyama, on t he bank of the Oigawa. Having wasted his substance in riotous living, this farmer made for himself, out of the mud in his garden, a clay-model of the *Mugen-Kane*; and he beat the clay-bell, and broke it, crying out the while for great wealth.

Then, out of the ground before him, rose up the figure of a white-robed woman, with long loose-flowing hair, holding a covered jar. And the woman said: "I have come to answer your fervent prayer as it deserves to be answered. Take, therefore, this jar." So saying, she put the jar into his hands, and disappeared.

Into his house the happy man rushed, to tell his

wife the good news. He set down in front of her the covered jar, which was heavy, and they opened it together. And they found that it was filled, up to the very brim, with...

But no! – *I really cannot tell you with what it was filled.*

NOTES

1. The two-hour period between 1 AM and 3 AM.

JIKININKI

Once, when Muso Kokushi, a priest of the Zen sect, was journeying alone through the province of Mino, he lost his way in a mountain-district where there was nobody to direct him. For a long time he wandered about helplessly; and he was beginning to despair of finding shelter for the night, when he perceived, on the top of a hill lighted by the last rays of the sun, one of those little hermitages, called *anjitsu*, which are built for solitary priests. It seemed to be in ruinous condition; but he hastened to it eagerly, and found that it was inhabited by an aged priest, from whom he begged the favour of a night's lodging. This the old man harshly refused; but he directed Muso to a certain hamlet, in the valley adjoining where lodging and food could be obtained.

Muso found his way to the hamlet, which consisted of less than a dozen farm-cottages; and he was kindly received at the dwelling of the headman. Forty or fifty persons were assembled in the principal apartment, at the moment of Muso's arrival; but he was shown into a small separate room, where he was promptly supplied with food and bedding. Being very tired, he lay down to rest at an early hour; but a little before midnight he was roused from sleep by a sound of loud weeping in the next apartment. Presently the sliding-screens were gently pushed apart; and a young man, carrying a lighted lantern, entered the room, respectfully saluted him, and said:

"Reverend Sir, it is my painful duty to tell you that I am now the responsible head of this house. Yesterday I was only the eldest son. But when you came here, tired as you were, we did not wish that you should feel embarrassed in any way: therefore we did not tell you that father had died only a few hours before. The people whom you saw in the next room are the inhabitants of this village: they all assembled here to pay their last respects to the dead; and now they are going to another village, about three miles off – for by our custom, no one of us may remain in this village during the night after a death has taken place. We make the proper offerings and prayers; then we go away, leaving the corpse alone. Strange things always happen in the house where a corpse has thus been left: so we think that it will be better for you to come away with us. We can find you good lodging in the other village. But perhaps, as you are a priest, you have no fear of demons or evil spirits; and, if you are not afraid of being left alone with the body, you will be very welcome to the use of this poor house. However, I must tell you that nobody, except a priest, would dare to remain here tonight."

Muso made answer:

"For your kind intention and your generous hospitality and am deeply grateful. But I am sorry that you did not tell me of your father's death when I came; for, though I was a little tired, I certainly was not so tired that I should have found difficulty in doing my duty as a priest. Had you told me, I could have performed the service before your departure. As it is, I shall perform the service after you have gone away; and I shall stay by the body until morning. I do not know what you mean by your words about the danger of staying here alone; but I am not afraid of ghosts or demons: therefore please to feel no anxiety on my account."

The young man appeared to be rejoiced by these assurances, and expressed his gratitude in fitting words. Then the other members of the family, and the folk assembled in the adjoining room, having been told of the priest's kind promises, came to thank him, after which the master of the house said:

"Now, reverend Sir, much as we regret to leave you alone, we must bid you farewell. By the rule of our village, none of us can stay here after midnight. We beg, kind Sir, that you will take every care of your honourable body, while we are unable to attend upon you. And if you happen to hear or see anything strange during our absence, please tell us of the matter when we return in the morning."

All then left the house, except the priest, who went to the room where the dead body was lying. The usual offerings had been set before the corpse; and a small Buddhist lamp – *tomyo* – was burning. The priest recited the service, and performed the funeral ceremonies, after which he entered into meditation. So meditating he remained through several silent hours; and there was no sound in the deserted village. But, when the hush of the night was at its deepest, there noiselessly entered a Shape, vague and vast; and in the same moment Muso found himself without power to move or speak. He saw that Shape lift the corpse, as with hands, devour it, more quickly than a cat devours a rat, beginning at the head, and eating everything: the hair and the bones and even the shroud. And the monstrous Thing, having thus consumed the body, turned to the offerings, and ate them also. Then it went away, as mysteriously as it had come.

When the villagers returned next morning, they found the priest awaiting them at the door of the headman's dwelling. All in turn saluted him; and when they had entered, and looked about the room, no one expressed any surprise at the disappearance of the dead body and the offerings. But the master of the house said to Muso:

"Reverent Sir, you have probably seen unpleasant things during the night: all of us were anxious about you. But now we are very happy to find you alive and unharmed. Gladly we would have stayed with you, if it had been possible. But the law of our village, as I told you last evening, obliges us to quit our houses after a death has taken place, and to leave the corpse alone. Whenever this law has been broken, heretofore, some great misfortune has followed. Whenever it is obeyed, we find that the corpse and the offerings disappear during our absence. Perhaps you have seen the cause."

Then Muso told of the dim and awful Shape that had entered the death-chamber to devour the body and the offerings. No person seemed to be surprised by his narration; and the master of the house observed:

"What you have told us, reverend Sir, agrees with what has been said about this matter from ancient time."

Muso then inquired:

"Does not the priest on the hill sometimes perform the funeral service for your dead?"

"What priest?" the young man asked.

"The priest who yesterday evening directed me to this village," answered Muso. "I called at his *anjitsu* on the hill yonder. He refused me lodging, but told me the way here."

The listeners looked at each other, as in astonishment; and, after a moment of silence, the master of the house said:

"Reverend Sir, there is no priest and there is no anjitsu on the hill. For the time of many generations there has not been any resident-priest in this neighbourhood."

Muso said nothing more on the subject; for it was evident that his kind hosts supposed him to have been deluded by some goblin. But after having bidden them farewell, and obtained all necessary information as to his road, he determined to look again for the hermitage on the hill, and so to ascertain whether he had really been deceived. He found the *anjitsu* without any difficulty; and, this time, its aged occupant invited him to enter. When he had done so, the hermit humbly bowed down before him, exclaiming: "Ah! I am ashamed! – I am very much ashamed! – I am exceedingly ashamed!"

"You need not be ashamed for having refused me shelter," said Muso. "You directed me to the village yonder, where I was very kindly treated; and I thank you for that favour.

"I can give no man shelter," the recluse made answer; and it is not for the refusal that I am ashamed. I am ashamed only that you should have seen me in my real shape – for it was I who devoured the corpse and the offerings last night before your eyes... Know, reverend Sir, that I am a *jikininki*[1] – an eater of human flesh. Have pity upon me, and suffer me to confess the secret fault by which I became reduced to this condition.

"A long, long time ago, I was a priest in this desolate region. There was no other priest for many leagues around. So, in that time, the bodies of the mountain-folk who died used to be brought here – sometimes from great distances – in order that I might repeat over them the holy service. But I repeated the service and performed the rites only as a matter of business; I thought only of the food and the clothes that my sacred profession enabled me to gain. And because of this selfish impiety I was reborn, immediately after my death, into the state of a *jikininki*. Since then I have been obliged to feed upon the corpses of the people who die in this district: every one of them I must devour in the way that you saw last night... Now, reverend Sir, let me beseech you to perform a *Segaki*-service for me: help me by your prayers, I entreat you, so that I may be soon able to escape from this horrible state of existence"...

No sooner had the hermit uttered this petition than he disappeared; and the hermitage also disappeared at the same instant. And Muso Kokushi found himself kneeling alone in the high grass, beside an ancient and moss-grown tomb of the form called *go-rin-ishi*,[2] which seemed to be the tomb of a priest.

NOTES

1. Literally, a man-eating goblin. The Japanese narrator gives also the Sanscrit term, "*Rakshasa*", but this word is quite as vague as *jikininki*, since there are many kinds of *Rakshasa*s. Apparently the word *jikininki* signifies here one of the *Baramon-Rasetsu-Gaki*, forming the twenty-sixth class of pretas enumerated in the old Buddhist books of Hell.

2. *Go-rinshi*: literally, "five-circle [or five-zone] stone." A funeral monument consisting of five parts superimposed, each of a different form, symbolizing the five mystic elements: Ether, Air, Fire, Water, Earth.

MUJINA

On the Akasaka Road, in Tokyo, there is a slope called Kii-no-kuni-zaka, which means the *Slope of the Province of Kii*. I do not know why it is called the Slope of the Province of Kii. On one side of this slope you see an ancient moat, deep and very wide, with high green banks rising up to some place of gardens; and on the other side of the road extend the long and lofty walls of an imperial palace. Before the era of street-lamps and jinrikishas, this neighbourhood was very lonesome after dark; and belated pedestrians would go miles out of their way rather than mount the Kii-no-kuni-zaka, alone, after sunset.

All because of a *mujina*[1] that used to walk there.

The last man who saw the *mujina* was an old merchant of the Kyobashi quarter, who died about thirty years ago. This is the story, as he told it:

One night, at a late hour, he was hurrying up the Kii-no-kuni-zaka, when he perceived a woman crouching by the moat, all alone, and weeping bitterly. Fearing that she intended to drown herself, he stopped to offer her any assistance or consolation in his power. She appeared to be a slight and graceful person, handsomely dressed; and her hair was arranged like that of a young girl of good family. "O-jochu," ["honourable maiden"] he exclaimed, approaching her, "O-jochu, do not cry like that!... Tell me what the trouble is; and if there be any way to help you, I shall be glad to help you." (He really meant what he said; for he was a very kind man.) But she continued to weep, hiding her face from him with one of her long sleeves. "O-jochu," he said again, as gently as he could, "please, please listen to me!... This is no place for a young lady at night! Do not cry, I implore you! – only tell me how I may be of some help to you!" Slowly she rose up, but turned her back to him, and continued to moan and sob behind her sleeve. He laid his hand lightly upon her shoulder, and pleaded: "O-jochu! – O-jochu! – O-jochu!... Listen to me, just for one little moment!... O-jochu! – O-jochu!"

Then that O-jochu turned around, and dropped her sleeve, and stroked her face with her hand; and the man saw that she had no eyes or nose or mouth, and he screamed and ran away.[2]

Up Kii-no-kuni-zaka he ran and ran; and all was black and empty before him. On and on he ran, never daring to look back; and at last he saw a lantern, so far away that it looked like the gleam of a firefly; and he made for it. It proved to be only the lantern of an itinerant *soba*-seller, who had set down his stand by the road-side; but any light and any human companionship was good after that experience; and he flung himself down at the feet of the *soba*-seller, crying out, "Ah! – aa!! – *aa!!!*"

"*Kore! kore!*" roughly exclaimed the *soba*-man. "Here! what is the matter with you? Anybody hurt you?"

"No – nobody hurt me," panted the other, "only...

Ah! – aa!"

"Only scared you?" queried the peddler, unsympathetically. "Robbers?"

"Not robbers, not robbers," gasped the terrified man... "I saw... I saw a woman – by the moat; and she showed me... Ah! I cannot tell you what she showed me!"...

"*He!* Was it anything like THIS that she showed you?" cried the *soba*-man, stroking his own face – which therewith became as smooth as an egg... and, simultaneously, the light went out.

NOTES

1. *Mujina*: a kind of goblin-badger (although in some regions the term refers instead to the Japanese raccoon dog, also called *tanuki*). Certain "witch-animals" were thought to be able to transform themselves and cause mischief for humans.

2. An apparition with a smooth, totally featureless face, called a *nopperabo*, is a stock form of *yokai*, from the Japanese pantheon of ghosts and demons.

ROKURO-KUBI

Nearly five hundred years ago there was a *samurai*, named Isogai Heidazaemon Taketsura, in the service of the Lord Kikuji, of Kyushu. This Isogai had inherited, from many warlike ancestors, a natural aptitude for military exercises, and extraordinary strength. While yet a boy he had surpassed his teachers in the art of swordsmanship, in archery, and in the use of the spear, and had displayed all the capacities of a daring and skillful soldier. Afterwards, in the time of the Eikyo war, he so distinguished himself that high honours were bestowed upon him. But when the house of Kikuji came to ruin, Isogai found himself without a master. He might then easily have obtained service under another daimyo; but as he had never sought distinction for his own sake alone, and as his heart remained true to his former lord, he preferred to give up the world. So he cut off his hair, and became a traveling priest, taking the Buddhist name of Kwairyo.

But always, under the *koromo*[1] of the priest, Kwairyo kept warm within him the heart of the *samurai*. As in other years he had laughed at peril, so now also he scorned danger; and in all weathers and all seasons he journeyed to preach the good Law in places where no other priest would have dared to go. For that age was an age of violence and disorder; and upon the highways there was no security for the solitary traveler, even if he happened to be a priest.

In the course of his first long journey, Kwairyo had occasion to visit the province of Kai. One evening, as he was traveling through the mountains of that province, darkness overcame him in a very lonesome district, leagues away from any village. So he resigned himself to pass the night under the stars; and having found a suitable grassy spot, by the roadside, he lay down there, and prepared to sleep. He had always welcomed discomfort; and even a bare rock was for him a good bed, when nothing better could be found, and the root of a pine-tree an excellent pillow. His body was iron; and he never troubled himself about dews or rain or frost or snow.

Scarcely had he lain down when a man came along the road, carrying an axe and a great bundle of chopped wood. This woodcutter halted on seeing Kwairyo lying down, and, after a moment of silent observation, said to him in a tone of great surprise:

"What kind of a man can you be, good Sir, that you dare to lie down alone in such a place as this?... There are haunters about here, many of them. Are you not afraid of Hairy Things?"

"My friend," cheerfully answered Kwairyo, "I am only a wandering priest, a 'Cloud-and-Water-Guest,' as folks call it: *Unsui-no-ryokaku*. And I am not in the least afraid of Hairy Things, if you mean goblin-foxes, or goblin-badgers, or any creatures of that kind. As for lonesome places, I like them: they are suitable for meditation. I am accustomed to sleeping in the open air: and I have learned never to be anxious about my life."

"You must be indeed a brave man, Sir Priest," the peasant responded, "to lie down here! This place has a bad name – a very bad name. But, as the proverb has it, *Kunshi ayayuki ni chikayorazu* ["The superior man does not needlessly expose himself to peril"]; and I must assure you, Sir, that it is very dangerous to sleep here. Therefore, although my house is only a wretched thatched hut, let me beg of you to come home with me at once. In the way of food, I have nothing to offer you; but there is a roof at least, and you can sleep under it without risk."

He spoke earnestly; and Kwairyo, liking the kindly tone of the man, accepted this modest offer. The woodcutter guided him along a narrow path, leading up from the main road through mountain-forest. It was a rough and dangerous path, sometimes skirting precipices, sometimes offering nothing but a network of slippery roots for the foot to rest upon, sometimes winding over or between masses of jagged rock. But at last Kwairyo found himself upon a cleared space at the top of a hill, with a full moon shining overhead; and he saw before him a small thatched cottage, cheerfully lighted from within. The woodcutter led him to a shed at the back of the house, whither water had been conducted, through bamboo-pipes, from some neighbouring stream; and the two men washed their feet. Beyond the shed was a vegetable garden, and a grove of cedars and bamboos; and beyond the trees appeared the glimmer of a cascade, pouring from some loftier height, and swaying in the moonshine like a long white robe.

As Kwairyo entered the cottage with his guide, he perceived four persons – men and women – warming their hands at a little fire kindled in the ro^2 of the principle apartment. They bowed low to the priest, and greeted him in the most respectful manner. Kwairyo wondered that persons so poor, and dwelling in such a solitude, should be aware of the polite forms of greeting. "These are good people," he thought to himself; "and they must have been taught by some one well acquainted with the rules of propriety." Then turning to his host – the *aruji*, or house-master, as the others called him – Kwairyo said:

"From the kindness of your speech, and from the very polite welcome given me by your household, I imagine that you have not always been a woodcutter. Perhaps you formerly belonged to one of the upper classes?"

Smiling, the woodcutter answered:

"Sir, you are not mistaken. Though now living as you find me, I was once a person of some distinction. My story is the story of a ruined life – ruined by my own fault. I used to be in the service of a *daimyo*; and my rank in that service was not inconsiderable. But I loved women and wine too well; and under the influence of passion I acted wickedly. My selfishness brought about the ruin of our house, and caused the death of many persons. Retribution followed me; and I long remained a fugitive in the land. Now I often pray that I may be able to make some atonement for the evil which I did, and to reestablish the ancestral home. But I fear that I shall never find any way of so doing. Nevertheless, I try to overcome the karma of my errors by sincere repentance, and by helping as afar as I can, those who are unfortunate."

Kwairyo was pleased by this announcement of good resolve; and he said to the *aruji*:

"My friend, I have had occasion to observe that man, prone to folly in their youth, may in after years become very earnest in right living. In the holy sutras it is written that those strongest in wrong-doing can become, by power of good resolve, the strongest in right-doing. I do not doubt that you have a good heart; and I hope that better fortune will come to you. tonight I shall recite the sutras for your sake, and pray that you may obtain the force to overcome the karma of any past errors."

With these assurances, Kwairyo bade the *aruji* good-night; and his host showed him to a very small side-room, where a bed had been made ready. Then all went to sleep except the priest, who began to read the sutras by the light of a paper lantern. Until a late hour he continued to read and pray: then he opened a little window in his little sleeping-room, to take a last look at the landscape before lying down. The night was beautiful: there was no cloud in the sky: there was no wind; and the strong moonlight threw down sharp black shadows of foliage, and glittered on the dews of the garden. Shrillings of crickets and bell-insects made a musical tumult; and the sound of the neighbouring cascade deepened with the night. Kwairyo felt thirsty as he listened to the noise of the water; and, remembering the bamboo aqueduct at the rear of the house, he thought that he could go there and get a drink without disturbing the sleeping household. Very gently he pushed apart the sliding-screens that separated his room from the main apartment; and he saw, by the light of the lantern, five recumbent bodies – without heads!

For one instant he stood bewildered, imagining a crime. But in another moment he perceived that there was no blood, and that the headless necks did not look as if they had been cut. Then he thought to himself: "Either this is an illusion made by goblins, or I have been lured into the dwelling of a *rokuro-kubi*...[3] In the book *Soshinki*[4] it is written that if one find the body of a *rokuro-kubi* without its head, and remove the body to another place, the head will never be able to join itself again to the neck. And the book further says that when the head comes back and finds that its body has been moved, it will strike itself upon the floor three times, bounding like a ball, and will pant as in great fear, and presently die. Now, if these be *rokuro-kubi*, they mean me no good; so I shall be justified in following the instructions of the book..."

He seized the body of the *aruji* by the feet, pulled it to the window, and pushed it out. Then he went to the back-door, which he found barred; and he surmised that the heads had made their exit through the smoke-hole in the roof, which had been left open. Gently unbarring the door, he made his way to the garden, and proceeded with all possible caution to the grove beyond it. He heard voices talking in the grove; and he went in the direction of the voices, stealing from shadow to shadow, until he reached a good hiding-place. Then, from behind a trunk, he caught sight of the heads, all five of them, flitting about, and chatting as they flitted. They were eating worms and insects which they found on the ground or among the trees. Presently the head of the aruji stopped eating and said:

"Ah, that traveling priest who came tonight! How fat all his body is! When we shall have eaten him, our bellies will be well filled... I was foolish to talk to him as I did; it only set him to reciting the sutras on behalf of my soul! To go near him while he is reciting would be difficult; and we cannot touch him so long as he is praying. But as it is now nearly morning, perhaps he has gone to sleep... Some one of you go to the house and see what the fellow is doing."

Another head – the head of a young woman – immediately rose up and flitted to the house, lightly as a bat. After a few minutes it came back, and cried out huskily, in a tone of great alarm:

"That traveling priest is not in the house; he is gone! But that is not the worst of the matter. He has taken the body of our *aruji*; and I do not know where he has put it."

At this announcement the head of the *aruji* – distinctly visible in the moonlight – assumed a frightful aspect: its eyes opened monstrously; its hair stood up bristling; and its teeth gnashed. Then a cry burst from its lips; and – weeping tears of rage – it exclaimed:

"Since my body has been moved, to rejoin it is not possible! Then I must die!... And all through the work of that priest! Before I die I will get at that priest! – I will tear him! – I will devour him!... AND THERE HE IS – behind that tree! – hiding behind that tree! See him! – the fat coward!"...

In the same moment the head of the *aruji*, followed by the other four heads, sprang at Kwairyo. But the strong priest had already armed himself by plucking up a young tree; and with that tree he struck the heads as they came, knocking them from him with tremendous blows. Four of them fled away. But the head of the aruji, though battered again and again, desperately continued to bound at the priest, and at last caught him by the left sleeve of his robe. Kwairyo, however, as quickly gripped the head by its topknot, and repeatedly struck it. It did not release its hold; but it uttered a long moan, and thereafter ceased to struggle. It was dead. But its teeth still held the sleeve; and, for all his great strength, Kwairyo could not force open the jaws.

With the head still hanging to his sleeve he went back to the house, and there caught sight of the other four *rokuro-kubi* squatting together, with their bruised and bleeding heads reunited to their bodies. But when they perceived him at the back-door all screamed, "The priest! the priest!" and fled, through the other doorway, out into the woods.

Eastward the sky was brightening; day was about to dawn; and Kwairyo knew that the power of the goblins was limited to the hours of darkness. He looked at the head clinging to his sleeve, its face all fouled with blood and foam and clay; and he laughed aloud as he thought to himself: "What a *miyage!*[5] – the head of a goblin!" After which he gathered together his few belongings, and leisurely descended the mountain to continue his journey.

Right on he journeyed, until he came to Suwa in Shinano; and into the main street of Suwa he solemnly strode, with the head dangling at his elbow. Then woman fainted, and children screamed and ran away; and there was a great crowding and clamouring until the *torite* (as the police in those days were called) seized the priest, and took him to jail. For they supposed the head to be the head of a murdered man who, in the moment of being killed, had caught the murderer's sleeve in his teeth. As the Kwairyo, he only smiled and said nothing when they questioned him. So, after having passed a night in prison, he was brought before the magistrates of the district. Then he was ordered to explain how he, a priest, had been found with the head of a man fastened to his sleeve, and why he had dared thus shamelessly to parade his crime in the sight of people.

Kwairyo laughed long and loudly at these questions; and then he said:

"Sirs, I did not fasten the head to my sleeve: it fastened itself there – much against my will. And I have not committed any crime. For this is not the head of a man; it is the head of a goblin; and, if I caused the death of the goblin, I did not do so by any shedding of blood, but simply by taking the precautions necessary to assure my own safety."... And he proceeded to relate the whole of the adventure, bursting into another hearty laugh as he told of his encounter with the five heads.

But the magistrates did not laugh. They judged him to be a hardened criminal, and his story an insult to their intelligence. Therefore, without any further questioning, they decided to order his immediate execution – all of them except one, a very old man. This aged officer had made no remark during the trial; but, after having heard the opinion of his colleagues, he rose up, and said:

"Let us first examine the head carefully; for this, I think, has not yet been done. If the priest has spoken truth, the head itself should bear witness for him... Bring the head here!"

So the head, still holding in its teeth the *koromo* that had been stripped from Kwairyo's shoulders, was put before the judges. The old man turned it round and round, carefully examined it, and discovered, on the nape of its neck, several strange red characters. He called the attention of his colleagues to these, and also bad them observe that the edges of the neck nowhere presented the appearance of having been cut by any weapon. On the contrary, the line of leverance was smooth as the line at which a falling leaf detaches itself from the stem... Then said the elder:

"I am quite sure that the priest told us nothing

but the truth. This is the head of a *rokuro-kubi*. In the book *Nan-ho-i-butsu-shi* it is written that certain red characters can always be found upon the nape of the neck of a real *rokuro-kubi*. There are the characters: you can see for yourselves that they have not been painted. Moreover, it is well known that such goblins have been dwelling in the mountains of the province of Kai from very ancient time... But you, Sir," he exclaimed, turning to Kwairyo, "what sort of sturdy priest may you be? Certainly you have given proof of a courage that few priests possess; and you have the air of a soldier rather than a priest. Perhaps you once belonged to the *samurai*-class?"

"You have guessed rightly, Sir," Kwairyo responded. "Before becoming a priest, I long followed the profession of arms; and in those days I never feared man or devil. My name then was Isogai Heidazaemon Taketsura of Kyushu: there may be some among you who remember it."

At the mention of that name, a murmur of admiration filled the court-room; for there were many present who remembered it. And Kwairyo immediately found himself among friends instead of judges, friends anxious to prove their admiration by fraternal kindness. With honour they escorted him to the residence of the daimyo, who welcomed him, and feasted him, and made him a handsome present before allowing him to depart. When Kwairyo left Suwa, he was as happy as any priest is permitted to be in this transitory world. As for the head, he took it with him, jocosely insisting that he intended it for a *miyage*.

And now it only remains to tell what became of the head.

A day or two after leaving Suwa, Kwairyo met with a robber, who stopped him in a lonesome place, and bade him strip. Kwairyo at once removed his koromo, and offered it to the robber, who then first perceived what was hanging to the sleeve. Though brave, the highwayman was startled: he dropped the garment, and sprang back. Then he cried out: "You! – what kind of a priest are you? Why, you are a worse man than I am! It is true that I have killed people; but I never walked about with anybody's head fastened to my sleeve... Well, Sir priest, I suppose we are of the same calling; and I must say that I admire you!... Now that head would be of use to me: I could frighten people with it. Will you sell it? You can have my robe in exchange for your *koromo*; and I will give you five *ryo* for the head."

Kwairyo answered:

"I shall let you have the head and the robe if you insist; but I must tell you that this is not the head of a man. It is a goblin's head. So, if you buy it, and have any trouble in consequence, please to remember that you were not deceived by me."

"What a nice priest you are!" exclaimed the robber. "You kill men, and jest about it!... But I am really in earnest. Here is my robe; and here is the money; and let me have the head... What is the use of joking?"

"Take the thing," said Kwairyo. "I was not joking. The only joke – if there be any joke at all – is that you are fool enough to pay good money for a goblin's head." And Kwairyo, loudly laughing, went upon his way.

Thus the robber got the head and the *koromo*; and for some time he played goblin-priest upon the highways. But, reaching the neighbourhood of Suwa, he there learned the true story of the head; and he then became afraid that the spirit of the *rokuro-kubi* might give him trouble. So he made up his mind to take back the head to the place from which it had come, and to bury it with its body. He found his way to the lonely cottage in the mountains of Kai; but nobody was there, and he could not discover the body. Therefore he buried the head by itself, in the grove behind the cottage; and he had a tombstone set up over the grave; and he caused a *Segaki*-service to be performed on behalf of the spirit of the *rokuro-kubi*. And that tombstone – known as the tombstone of the *rokuro-kubi* – may be seen (at least so the Japanese story-teller declares) even unto this day.

NOTES

1. *Koromo*: the upper robe of a Buddhist priest.

2. *Ro*: a sort of little fireplace, contrived in the floor of a room. The *ro* is usually a square shallow cavity, lined with metal and half-filled with ashes, in which charcoal is lighted.

3. A *rokuro-kubi* is ordinarily conceived as a goblin whose neck stretches out to great lengths, but which nevertheless always remains attached to its body.

4. A Chinese collection of stories on the supernatural.

5. A present made to friends or to the household on returning from a journey. Ordinarily, of course, the *miyage* consists of something produced in the locality to which the journey has been made: this is the point of Kwairyo's jest.

A DEAD SECRET

A long time ago, in the province of Tamba, there lived a rich merchant named Inamuraya Gensuke. He had a daughter called O-Sono. As she was very clever and pretty, he thought it would be a pity to let her grow up with only such teaching as the country-teachers could give her: so he sent her, in care of some trusty attendants, to Kyoto, that she might be trained in the polite accomplishments taught to the ladies of the capital. After she had thus been educated, she was married to a friend of her father's family, a merchant named Nagaraya; and she lived happily with him for nearly four years. They had one child, a son, but O-Sono fell ill and died, in the fourth year after her marriage.

On the night after the funeral of O-Sono, her little son said that his mamma had come back, and was in the room upstairs. She had smiled at him, but would not talk to him: so he became afraid, and ran away. Then some of the family went upstairs to the room which had been O-Sono's; and they were startled to see, by the light of a small lamp which had been kindled before a shrine in that room, the figure of the dead mother. She appeared as if standing in front of a *tansu*, or chest of drawers, that still contained her ornaments and her wearing-apparel. Her head and shoulders could be very distinctly seen; but from the waist downwards the figure thinned into invisibility; it was like an imperfect reflection of her, and transparent as a shadow on water.

Then the folk were afraid, and left the room. Below they consulted together; and the mother of O-Sono's husband said: "A woman is fond of her small things; and O-Sono was much attached to her belongings. Perhaps she has come back to look at them. Many dead persons will do that, unless the things be given to the parish-temple. If we present O-Sono's robes and girdles to the temple, her spirit will probably find rest."

It was agreed that this should be done as soon as possible. So on the following morning the drawers were emptied; and all of O-Sono's ornaments and dresses were taken to the temple. But she came back the next night, and looked at the *tansu* as before. And she came back also on the night following, and the night after that, and every night; and the house became a house of fear.

The mother of O-Sono's husband then went to the parish-temple, and told the chief priest all that had happened, and asked for ghostly counsel. The temple was a Zen temple; and the head-priest was a learned old man, known as Daigen Osho. He said: "There must be something about which she is anxious, in or near that *tansu*." – "But we emptied all the drawers," replied the woman; "there is nothing in the *tansu*." – "Well," said Daigen Osho, "tonight I shall go to your house, and keep watch in that room, and see what can be done. You must give orders that no person shall enter the room while I am watching, unless I call."

After sundown, Daigen Osho went to the house, and found the room made ready for him. He remained there alone, reading the sutras; and nothing appeared until after the Hour of the Rat.[1] Then the figure of O-Sono suddenly outlined itself in front of the *tansu*. Her face had a wistful look; and she kept her eyes fixed upon the tansu.

The priest uttered the holy formula prescribed in such cases, and then, addressing the figure by the *kaimyo*[2] of O-Sono, said: "I have come here in order to help you. Perhaps in that *tansu* there is something about which you have reason to feel anxious. Shall I try to find it for you?" The shadow appeared to give assent by a slight motion of the head; and the priest, rising, opened the top drawer. It was empty. Successively he opened the second, the third, and the fourth drawer; he searched carefully behind them and beneath them; he carefully examined the interior of the chest. He found nothing. But the figure remained gazing as wistfully as before. "What can she want?" thought the priest. Suddenly it occurred to him that there might be something hidden under the paper with which the drawers were lined. He removed the lining of the first drawer – nothing! He removed the lining of the second and third drawers – still nothing. But under the lining of the lowermost drawer, he found a letter. "Is this the thing about which you have been troubled?" he asked. The shadow of the woman turned toward him, her faint gaze fixed upon the letter. "Shall I burn it for you?" he asked. She bowed before him. "It shall be burned in the temple this very morning," he promised; "and no one shall read it, except myself." The figure smiled and vanished.

Dawn was breaking as the priest descended the stairs, to find the family waiting anxiously below. "Do not be anxious," he said to them; "she will not appear again." And she never did.

The letter was burned. It was a love-letter written to O-Sono in the time of her studies at Kyoto. But the priest alone knew what was in it; and the secret died with him.

NOTES

1. The Hour of the Rat (*ne-no-koku*), according to the old Japanese method of reckoning time, was the first hour. It corresponded to the time between our midnight and two o'clock in the morning; for the ancient Japanese hours were each equal to two modern hours.

2. *Kaimyo*, the posthumous Buddhist name, or religious name, given to the dead.

YUKI-ONNA

In a village of Musashi Province, there lived two woodcutters: Mosaku and Minokichi. At the time of which I am speaking, Mosaku was an old man; and Minokichi, his apprentice, was a lad of eighteen years. Every day they went together to a forest situated about five miles from their village. On the way to that forest there is a wide river to cross; and there is a ferry-boat. Several times a bridge was built where the ferry is; but the bridge was each time carried away by a flood. No common bridge can resist the current there when the river rises.

Mosaku and Minokichi were on their way home, one very cold evening, when a great snowstorm overtook them. They reached the ferry; and they found that the boatman had gone away, leaving his boat on the other side of the river. It was no day for swimming; and the woodcutters took shelter in the ferryman's hut, thinking themselves lucky to find any shelter at all. There was no brazier in the hut, nor any place in which to make a fire: it was only a two-mat hut, with a single door, but no window. Mosaku and Minokichi fastened the door, and lay down to rest, with their straw rain-coats over them. At first they did not feel very cold; and they thought that the storm would soon be over.

The old man almost immediately fell asleep; but

the boy, Minokichi, lay awake a long time, listening to the awful wind, and the continual slashing of the snow against the door. The river was roaring; and the hut swayed and creaked like a junk at sea. It was a terrible storm; and the air was every moment becoming colder; and Minokichi shivered under his rain-coat. But at last, in spite of the cold, he too fell asleep.

He was awakened by a showering of snow in his face. The door of the hut had been forced open; and, by the snow-light [*yuki-akari*], he saw a woman in the room, a woman all in white. She was bending above Mosaku, and blowing her breath upon him; and her breath was like a bright white smoke. Almost in the same moment she turned to Minokichi, and stooped over him. He tried to cry out, but found that he could not utter any sound. The white woman bent down over him, lower and lower, until her face almost touched him; and he saw that she was very beautiful, though her eyes made him afraid. For a little time she continued to look at him; then she smiled, and she whispered: "I intended to treat you like the other man. But I cannot help feeling some pity for you, because you are so young... You are a pretty boy, Minokichi; and I will not hurt you now. But, if you ever tell anybody – even your own mother – about what you have seen this night, I shall know it; and then I will kill you... Remember what I say!"

With these words, she turned from him, and passed through the doorway. Then he found himself able to move; and he sprang up, and looked out. But the woman was nowhere to be seen; and the snow was driving furiously into the hut. Minokichi closed the door, and secured it by fixing several billets of wood against it. He wondered if the wind had blown it open; he thought that he might have been only dreaming, and might have mistaken the gleam of the snow-light in the doorway for the figure of a white woman: but he could not be sure. He called to Mosaku, and was frightened because the old man did not answer. He put out his hand in the dark, and touched Mosaku's face, and found that it was ice! Mosaku was stark and dead...

By dawn the storm was over; and when the ferryman returned to his station, a little after sunrise, he found Minokichi lying senseless beside the frozen body of Mosaku. Minokichi was promptly cared for, and soon came to himself; but he remained a long time ill from the effects of the cold of that terrible night. He had been greatly frightened also by the old man's death; but he said nothing about the vision of the woman in white. As soon as he got well again, he returned to his calling, going alone every morning to the forest, and coming back at nightfall with his bundles of wood, which his mother helped him to sell.

One evening, in the winter of the following year, as he was on his way home, he overtook a girl who happened to be traveling by the same road. She was a tall, slim girl, very good-looking; and she answered Minokichi's greeting in a voice as pleasant to the ear as the voice of a song-bird. Then he walked beside her; and they began to talk. The girl said that her name was O-Yuki; that she had lately lost both of her parents; and that she was going to Edo, where she happened to have some poor relations, who might help her to find a situation as a servant. Minokichi soon felt charmed by this strange girl; and the more that he looked at her, the handsomer she appeared to be. He asked her whether she was yet betrothed; and she answered, laughingly, that she was free. Then, in her turn, she asked Minokichi whether he was married, or pledge to marry; and he told her that, although he had only a widowed mother to support, the question of an "honourable daughter-in-law" had not yet been considered, as he was very young... After these confidences, they walked on for a long while without speaking; but, as the proverb declares, *Ki ga areba, me mo kuchi hodo ni mono wo iu*: "When the wish is there, the eyes can say as much as the mouth." By the time they reached the village, they had become very much pleased with each other; and then Minokichi asked O-Yuki to rest awhile at his house. After some shy hesitation, she went there with him; and his mother made her welcome, and prepared a warm meal for her. O-Yuki behaved so nicely that Minokichi's mother took a sudden fancy to her, and persuaded her to delay her journey to Edo. And the natural end of the matter was that Yuki never went to Edo at all. She remained in the house, as an "honourable daughter-in-law".

O-Yuki proved a very good daughter-in-law. When Minokichi's mother came to die, some five years later, her last words were words of affection and praise for the wife of her son. And O-Yuki bore Minokichi ten children, boys and girls, handsome children all of them, and very fair of skin.

The country-folk thought O-Yuki a wonderful person, by nature different from themselves. Most of the peasant-women age early; but O-Yuki, even after having become the mother of ten children, looked as young and fresh as on the day when she had first come to the village.

One night, after the children had gone to sleep, O-Yuki was sewing by the light of a paper lamp; and Minokichi, watching her, said:

"To see you sewing there, with the light on your face, makes me think of a strange thing that happened when I was a lad of eighteen. I then saw somebody as beautiful and white as you are now – indeed, she was very like you."...

Without lifting her eyes from her work, O-Yuki responded:

"Tell me about her... Where did you see her?"

Then Minokichi told her about the terrible night in the ferryman's hut, and about the White Woman that had stooped above him, smiling and whispering, and about the silent death of old Mosaku. And he said:

"Asleep or awake, that was the only time that I saw a being as beautiful as you. Of course, she was not a human being; and I was afraid of her, very much afraid – but she was so white!... Indeed, I have never been sure whether it was a dream that I saw, or the Woman of the Snow..."

O-Yuki flung down her sewing, and arose, and

bowed above Minokichi where he sat, and shrieked into his face:

"It was I – I – I! Yuki it was! And I told you then that I would kill you if you ever said one work about it!... But for those children asleep there, I would kill you this moment! And now you had better take very, very good care of them; for if ever they have reason to complain of you, I will treat you as you deserve!"

Even as she screamed, her voice became thin, like a crying of wind; then she melted into a bright white mist that spired to the roof-beams, and shuddered away through the smoke-hold... Never again was she seen.

THE STORY OF AOYAGI

In the era of Bummei [1469-1486] there was a young *samurai* called Tomotada in the service of Hatakeyama Yoshimune, the Lord of Noto. Tomotada was a native of Echizen; but at an early age he had been taken, as page, into the palace of the daimyo of Noto, and had been educated, under the supervision of that prince, for the profession of arms. As he grew up, he proved himself both a good scholar and a good soldier, and continued to enjoy the favour of his prince. Being gifted with an amiable character, a winning address, and a very handsome person, he was admired and much liked by his *samurai*-comrades.

When Tomotada was about twenty years old, he was sent upon a private mission to Hosokawa Masamoto, the great daimyo of Kyoto, a kinsman of Hatakeyama Yoshimune. Having been ordered to journey through Echizen, the youth requested and obtained permission to pay a visit, on the way, to his widowed mother.

It was the coldest period of the year when he started; and, though mounted upon a powerful horse, he found himself obliged to proceed slowly. The road which he followed passed through a mountain-district where the settlements were few and far between; and on the second day of his journey, after a weary ride of hours, he was dismayed to find that he could not reached his intended halting-place until late in the night. He had reason to be anxious; for a heavy snowstorm came on, with an intensely cold wind; and the horse showed signs of exhaustion. But in that trying moment, Tomotada unexpectedly perceived the thatched room of a cottage on the summit of a near hill, where willow-trees were growing. With difficulty he urged his tired animal to the dwelling; and he loudly knocked upon the storm-doors, which had been closed against the wind. An old woman opened them, and cried out compassionately at the sight of the handsome stranger: "Ah, how pitiful! A young gentleman traveling alone in such weather!... Deign, young master, to enter."

Tomotada dismounted, and after leading his horse to a shed in the rear, entered the cottage, where he saw an old man and a girl warming themselves by a fire of bamboo splints. They respectfully invited him to approach the fire; and the old folks then proceeded to warm some rice-wine, and to prepare food for the traveler, whom they ventured to question in regard to his journey. Meanwhile the young girl disappeared behind a screen. Tomotada had observed, with astonishment, that she was extremely beautiful, though her attire was of the most wretched kind, and her long, loose hair in disorder. He wondered that so handsome a girl should be living in such a miserable and lonesome place.

The old man said to him:

"Honoured Sir, the next village is far; and the snow is falling thickly. The wind is piercing; and the road is very bad. Therefore, to proceed further this night would probably be dangerous. Although this hovel is unworthy of your presence, and although we have not any comfort to offer, perhaps it were safer to remain tonight under this miserable roof... We would take good care of your horse."

Tomotada accepted this humble proposal, secretly glad of the chance thus afforded him to see more of the young girl. Presently a coarse but ample meal was set before him; and the girl came from behind the screen, to serve the wine. She was now reclad, in a rough but cleanly robe of homespun; and her long, loose hair had been neatly combed and smoothed. As she bent forward to fill his cup, Tomotada was amazed to perceive that she was incomparably more beautiful than any woman whom he had ever before seen; and there was a grace about her every motion that astonished him. But the elders began to apologize for her, saying: "Sir, our daughter, Aoyagi, has been brought up here in the mountains, almost alone; and she knows nothing of gentle service. We pray that you will pardon her stupidity and her ignorance." Tomotada protested that he deemed himself lucky to be waited upon by so comely a maiden. He could not turn his eyes away from her – though he saw that his admiring gaze made her blush – and he left the wine and food untasted before him. The mother said: "Kind Sir, we very much hope that you will try to eat and to drink a little – though our peasant-fare is of the worst – as you must have been chilled by that piercing wind." Then, to please the old folks, Tomotada ate and drank as he could; but the charm of the blushing girl still grew upon him.

He talked with her, and found that her speech was sweet as her face. Brought up in the mountains as she might have been; but, in that case, her parents must at some time been persons of high degree; for she spoke and moved like a damsel of rank. Suddenly he addressed her with a poem – which was also a question – inspired by the delight in his heart:

> *Tadzunetsuru,*
> *Hana ka tote koso,*
> *Hi wo kurase,*
> *Akenu ni otoru*
> *Akane sasuran?*

["Being on my way to pay a visit, I found that which I took to be a flower: therefore here I spend the day... Why, in the time before dawn, the dawn-blush tint should glow – that, indeed, I know not."]

Without a moment's hesitation, she answered him in these verses:

> *Izuru hi no*
> *Honomeku iro wo*
> *Waga sode ni*
> *Tsutsumaba asu mo*
> *Kimiya tomaran.*

["If with my sleeve I hid the faint fair colour of the dawning sun – then, perhaps, in the morning my lord will remain."]

Then Tomotada knew that she accepted his admiration; and he was scarcely less surprised by the art with which she had uttered her feelings in verse, than delighted by the assurance which the verses conveyed. He was now certain that in all this world he could not hope to meet, much less to win, a girl more beautiful and witty than this rustic maid before him; and a voice in his heart seemed to cry out urgently, "Take the luck that the gods have put in your way!" In short he was bewitched – bewitched to such a degree that, without further preliminary, he asked the old people to give him their daughter in marriage – telling them, at the same time, his name and lineage, and his rank in the train of the Lord of Noto.

They bowed down before him, with many exclamations of grateful astonishment. But, after some moments of apparent hesitation, the father replied:

"Honoured master, you are a person of high position, and likely to rise to still higher things. Too great is the favour that you deign to offer us; indeed, the depth of our gratitude therefor is not to be spoken or measured. But this girl of ours, being a stupid country-girl of vulgar birth, with no training or teaching of any sort, it would be improper to let her become the wife of a noble *samurai*. Even to speak of such a matter is not right... But, since you find the girl to your liking, and have condescended to pardon her peasant-manners and to overlook her great rudeness, we do gladly present her to you, for an humble handmaid. Deign, therefore, to act hereafter in her regard according to your august pleasure."

Ere morning the storm had passed; and day broke through a cloudless east. Even if the sleeve of Aoyagi hid from her lover's eyes the rose-blush of that dawn, he could no longer tarry. But neither could he resign himself to part with the girl; and, when everything had been prepared for his journey, he thus addressed her parents:

"Though it may seem thankless to ask for more than I have already received, I must again beg you to give me your daughter for wife. It would be difficult for me to separate from her now; and as she is willing to accompany me, if you permit, I can take her with me as she is. If you will give her to me, I shall ever cherish you as parents... And, in the meantime, please to accept this poor acknowledgment of your kindest hospitality."

So saying, he placed before his humble host a purse of gold *ryo*. But the old man, after many prostrations, gently pushed back the gift, and said:

"Kind master, the gold would be of no use to us; and you will probably have need of it during your long, cold journey. Here we buy nothing; and we could not spend so much money upon ourselves, even if we wished... As for the girl, we have already bestowed her as a free gift; she belongs to you: therefore it is not necessary to ask our leave to take her away. Already she has told us that she hopes to accompany you, and to remain your servant for as long as you may be willing to endure her presence. We are only too happy to know that you deign to accept her; and we pray that you will not trouble yourself on our account. In this place we could not provide her with proper clothing, much less with a dowry. Moreover, being old, we should in any event have to separate from her before long. Therefore it is very fortunate that you should be willing to take her with you now."

It was in vain that Tomotada tried to persuade the old people to accept a present: he found that they cared nothing for money. But he saw that they were really anxious to trust their daughter's fate to his hands; and he therefore decided to take her with him. So he placed her upon his horse, and bade the old folks farewell for the time being, with many sincere expressions of gratitude.

"Honoured Sir," the father made answer, "it is we, and not you, who have reason for gratitude. We are sure that you will be kind to our girl; and we have no fears for her sake."...

[*Here, in the Japanese original, there is a queer break in the natural course of the narration, which therefrom remains curiously inconsistent. Nothing further is said about the mother of Tomotada, or about the parents of Aoyagi, or about the* daimyo *of Noto. Evidently the writer wearied of his work at this point, and hurried the story, very carelessly, to its startling end. I am not able to supply his omissions, or to repair his faults of construction; but I must venture to put in a few explanatory details, without which the rest of the tale would not hold together... It appears that Tomotada rashly took Aoyagi with him to Kyoto, and so got into trouble; but we are not informed as to where the couple lived afterwards.*]

...Now a *samurai* was not allowed to marry without the consent of his lord; and Tomotada could not expect to obtain this sanction before his mission had been accomplished. He had reason, under such circumstances, to fear that the beauty of Aoyagi might attract dangerous attention, and that means might be devised of taking her away from him. In Kyoto he therefore tried to keep her hidden from curious eyes. But a retainer of Lord Hosokawa one day caught sight of Aoyagi, discovered her relation to Tomotada, and reported the matter to the daimyo. Thereupon the *daimyo* – a young prince, and fond of pretty faces – gave orders that the girl should be brought to the place; and she was taken thither at once, without ceremony.

Tomotada sorrowed unspeakably; but he knew himself powerless. He was only an humble messenger in the service of a far-off *daimyo*; and for the time being he was at the mercy of a much more powerful *daimyo*, whose wishes were not to be questioned. Moreover Tomotada knew that he had acted foolishly, that he had brought about his own misfortune, by entering into a clandestine relation which the code of the military class condemned. There was now but one hope for him, a desperate hope: that Aoyagi might be able and willing to escape and to flee with him. After long reflection, he resolved to try to send her a letter. The attempt would be dangerous, of course: any writing sent to her might find its way to the hands of the *daimyo*; and to send a love-letter to any inmate of the place was an unpardonable offense. But he resolved to dare the risk; and, in the form of a Chinese poem, he composed a letter which he endeavored to have conveyed to her. The poem was written with only twenty-eight characters. But with those twenty-eight characters he was about to express all the depth of his passion, and to suggest all the pain of his loss:

> *Koshi o-son gojin wo ou;*
> *Ryokuju namida wo tarete rakin wo hitataru;*
> *Komon hitotabi irite fukaki koto umi no gotoshi;*
> *Kore yori shoro kore rojin*

["Closely, closely the youthful prince now follows after the gem-bright maid; The tears of the fair one, falling, have moistened all her robes. But the august lord, having once become enamoured of her – the depth of his longing is like the depth of the sea. Therefore it is only I that am left forlorn, only I that am left to wander alone."]

On the evening of the day after this poem had been sent, Tomotada was summoned to appear before the Lord Hosokawa. The youth at once suspected that his confidence had been betrayed; and he could not hope, if his letter had been seen by the *daimyo*, to escape the severest penalty. "Now he will order my death," thought Tomotada; "but I do not care to live unless Aoyagi be restored to me. Besides, if the death-sentence be passed, I can at least try to kill Hosokawa." He slipped his swords into his girdle, and hastened to the palace.

On entering the presence-room he saw the Lord Hosokawa seated upon the dais, surrounded by *samurai* of high rank, in caps and robes of ceremony. All were silent as statues; and while Tomotada advanced to make obeisance, the hush seemed to his sinister and heavy, like the stillness before a storm. But Hosokawa suddenly descended from the dais, and, while taking the youth by the arm, began to repeat the words of the poem: "*Koshi o-son gojin wo ou...*" And Tomotada, looking up, saw kindly tears in the prince's eyes.

Then said Hosokawa:

"Because you love each other so much, I have taken it upon myself to authorize your marriage, in lieu of my kinsman, the Lord of Noto; and your wedding shall now be celebrated before me. The guests are assembled; the gifts are ready."

At a signal from the lord, the sliding-screens concealing a further apartment were pushed open; and Tomotada saw there many dignitaries of the court, assembled for the ceremony, and Aoyagi awaiting him in brides' apparel... Thus was she given back to him; and the wedding was joyous and splendid; and precious gifts were made to the young couple by the prince, and by the members of his household.

For five happy years, after that wedding,

Tomotada and Aoyagi dwelt together. But one morning Aoyagi, while talking with her husband about some household matter, suddenly uttered a great cry of pain, and then became very white and still. After a few moments she said, in a feeble voice: "Pardon me for thus rudely crying out – but the paid was so sudden!... My dear husband, our union must have been brought about through some Karma-relation in a former state of existence; and that happy relation, I think, will bring us again together in more than one life to come. But for this present existence of ours, the relation is now ended; we are about to be separated. Repeat for me, I beseech you, the *Nembutsu*-prayer, because I am dying."

"Oh! what strange wild fancies!" cried the startled husband, "you are only a little unwell, my dear one!... lie down for a while, and rest; and the sickness will pass."...

"No, no!" she responded, "I am dying! – I do not imagine it – I know!... And it were needless now, my dear husband, to hide the truth from you any longer: I am not a human being. The soul of a tree is my soul; the heart of a tree is my heart; the sap of the willow is my life. And some one, at this cruel moment, is cutting down my tree; that is why I must die!... Even to weep were now beyond my strength! – quickly, quickly repeat the *Nembutsu* for me... quickly!... Ah!..."

With another cry of pain she turned aside her beautiful head, and tried to hide her face behind her sleeve. But almost in the same moment her whole form appeared to collapse in the strangest way, and to sank down, down, down – level with the floor. Tomotada had spring to support her; but there was nothing to support! There lay on the matting only the empty robes of the fair creature and the ornaments that she had worn in her hair: the body had ceased to exist...

Tomotada shaved his head, took the Buddhist vows, and became an itinerant priest. He travelled through all the provinces of the empire; and, at holy places which he visited, he offered up prayers for the soul of Aoyagi. Reaching Echizen, in the course of his pilgrimage, he sought the home of the parents of his beloved. But when he arrived at the lonely place among the hills, where their dwelling had been, he found that the cottage had disappeared. There was nothing to mark even the spot where it had stood, except the stumps of three willows – two old trees and one young tree – that had been cut down long before his arrival.

Beside the stumps of those willow-trees he erected a memorial tomb, inscribed with diverse holy texts; and he there performed many Buddhist services on behalf of the spirits of Aoyagi and of her parents.

JIU-ROKU-ZAKURA

In Wakegori, a district of the province of Iyo, there is a very ancient and famous cherry-tree, called *Jiu-roku-zakura*, or "the Cherry-tree of the Sixteenth Day", because it blooms every year upon the sixteenth day of the first month (by the old lunar calendar), and only upon that day. Thus the time of its flowering is the Period of Great Cold, though the natural habit of a cherry-tree is to wait for the spring season before venturing to blossom. But the *Jiu-roku-zakura* blossoms with a life that is not – or, at least, that was not originally – its own. There is the ghost of a man in that tree.

He was a *samurai* of Iyo; and the tree grew in his garden; and it used to flower at the usual time – that is to say, about the end of March or the beginning of April. He had played under that tree when he was a child; and his parents and grandparents and ancestors had hung to its blossoming branches, season after season for more than a hundred years, bright strips of coloured paper inscribed with poems of praise. He himself became very old, outliving all his children; and there was nothing in the world left for him to live except that tree. And lo! in the summer of a certain year, the tree withered and died!

Exceedingly the old man sorrowed for his tree. Then kind neighbours found for him a young and beautiful cherry-tree, and planted it in his garden, hoping thus to comfort him. And he thanked them, and pretended to be glad. But really his heart was full of pain; for he had loved the old tree so well that nothing could have consoled him for the loss of it.

At last there came to him a happy thought: he remembered a way by which the perishing tree might be saved. (It was the sixteenth day of the first month.) Along he went into his garden, and bowed down before the withered tree, and spoke to it, saying: "Now deign, I beseech you, once more to bloom, because I am going to die in your stead." (For it is believed that one can really give away one's life to another person, or to a creature or even to a tree, by the favour of the gods; and thus to transfer one's life is expressed by the term *migawari ni tatsu*, "to act as a substitute".) Then under that tree he spread a white cloth, and diveres coverings, and sat down upon the coverings, and performed *hara-kiri* after the fashion of a *samurai*. And the ghost of him went into the tree, and made it blossom in that same hour.

And every year it still blooms on the sixteenth day of the first month, in the season of snow.

THE DREAM OF AKINOSUKE

In the district called Toichi of Yamato Province, there
used to live a *goshi*[1] named Miyata Akinosuke. In
Akinosuke's garden there was a great and ancient cedar-
tree, under which he was wont to rest on sultry days.
One very warm afternoon he was sitting under this tree
with two of his friends, fellow-*goshi*, chatting and
drinking wine, when he felt all of a sudden very drowsy
– so drowsy that he begged his friends to excuse him for
taking a nap in their presence. Then he lay down at the
foot of the tree, and dreamed this dream:

He thought that as he was lying there in his
garden, he saw a procession, like the train of some great
daimyo descending a hill near by, and that he got up to
look at it. A very grand procession it proved to be, more
imposing than anything of the kind which he had ever
seen before; and it was advancing toward his dwelling.
He observed in the van of it a number of young men
richly appareled, who were drawing a great lacquered
palace-carriage, or *gosho-guruma*, hung with bright
blue silk. When the procession arrived within a short
distance of the house it halted; and a richly dressed man
– evidently a person of rank – advanced from it,
approached Akinosuke, bowed to him profoundly, and
then said:

"Honoured Sir, you see before you a *kerai*

["vassal"] of the Kokuo of Tokoyo.[2] My master, the King, commands me to greet you in his august name, and to place myself wholly at your disposal. He also bids me inform you that he augustly desires your presence at the palace. Be therefore pleased immediately to enter this honourable carriage, which he has sent for your conveyance."

Upon hearing these words Akinosuke wanted to make some fitting reply; but he was too much astonished and embarrassed for speech; and in the same moment his will seemed to melt away from him, so that he could only do as the *kerai* bade him. He entered the carriage; the kerai took a place beside him, and made a signal; the drawers, seizing the silken ropes, turned the great vehicle southward; and the journey began.

In a very short time, to Akinosuke's amazement, the carriage stopped in front of a huge two-storeyed gateway (*romon*), of a Chinese style, which he had never before seen. Here the kerai dismounted, saying, "I go to announce the honourable arrival," and he disappeared. After some little waiting, Akinosuke saw two noble-looking men, wearing robes of purple silk and high caps of the form indicating lofty rank, come from the gateway. These, after having respectfully saluted him, helped him to descend from the carriage, and led him through the great gate and across a vast garden, to the entrance of a palace whose front appeared to extend, west and east, to a distance of miles. Akinosuke was then shown into a reception-room of wonderful size and splendour. His guides conducted him to the place of honour, and respectfully seated themselves apart; while serving-maids, in costume of ceremony, brought refreshments. When Akinosuke had partaken of the refreshments, the two purple-robed attendants bowed low before him, and addressed him in the following words, each speaking alternately, according to the etiquette of courts:

"It is now our honourable duty to inform you... as to the reason of your having been summoned hither... Our master, the King, augustly desires that you become his son-in-law; and it is his wish and command that you shall wed this very day... the August Princess, his maiden-daughter... We shall soon conduct you to the presence-chamber... where His Augustness even now is waiting to receive you... But it will be necessary that we first invest you... with the appropriate garments of ceremony."

Having thus spoken, the attendants rose together, and proceeded to an alcove containing a great chest of gold lacquer. They opened the chest, and took from it various roes and girdles of rich material, and a *kamuri*, or regal headdress. With these they attired Akinosuke as befitted a princely bridegroom; and he was then conducted to the presence-room, where he saw the Kokuo of Tokoyo seated upon the *daiza* ["throne"], wearing a high black cap of state, and robed in robes of yellow silk. Before the *daiza*, to left and right, a multitude of dignitaries sat in rank, motionless and splendid as images in a temple; and Akinosuke, advancing into their midst, saluted the king with the triple prostration of usage. The king greeted him with gracious words, and then said:

"You have already been informed as to the reason of your having been summoned to Our presence. We have decided that you shall become the adopted husband of our only daughter; and the wedding ceremony shall now be performed."

As the king finished speaking, a sound of joyful music was heard; and a long train of beautiful court ladies advanced from behind a curtain to conduct Akinosuke to the room in which he bride awaited him.

The room was immense; but it could scarcely contain the multitude of guests assembled to witness the wedding ceremony. All bowed down before Akinosuke as he took his place, facing the King's daughter, on the kneeling-cushion prepared for him. As a maiden of heaven the bride appeared to be; and her robes were beautiful as a summer sky. And the marriage was performed amid great rejoicing.

Afterwards the pair were conducted to a suite of apartments that had been prepared for them in another portion of the palace; and there they received the congratulations of many noble persons, and wedding gifts beyond counting.

Some days later Akinosuke was again summoned to the throne-room. On this occasion he received even more graciously than before; and the King said to him:

"In the southwestern part of Our dominion there is an island called Raishu. We have now appointed you Governor of that island. You will find the people loyal and docile; but their laws have not yet been brought into proper accord with the laws of Tokoyo; and their customs have not been properly regulated. We entrust you with the duty of improving their social condition as far as may be possible; and We desire that you shall rule them with kindness and wisdom. All preparations necessary for your journey to Raishu have already been made."

So Akinosuke and his bride departed from the palace of Tokoyo, accompanied to the shore by a great escort of nobles and officials; and they embarked upon a ship of state provided by the king. And with favouring winds they safety sailed to Raishu, and found the good people of that island assembled upon the beach to welcome them.

Akinosuke entered at once upon his new duties; and they did not prove to be hard. During the first three years of his governorship he was occupied chiefly with the framing and the enactment of laws; but he had wise counselors to help him, and he never found the work unpleasant. When it was all finished, he had no active duties to perform, beyond attending the rites and ceremonies ordained by ancient custom. The country was so healthy and so fertile that sickness and want were unknown; and the people were so good that no laws were ever broken. And Akinosuke dwelt and ruled in Raishu for twenty years more, making in all twenty-three years of sojourn, during which no shadow of sorrow traversed his life.

But in the twenty-fourth year of his governorship, a great misfortune came upon him; for his wife, who had borne him seven children, five boys and two girls, fell sick and died. She was buried, with high pomp, on the summit of a beautiful hill in the district of Hanryoko; and a monument, exceedingly splendid, was placed upon her grave. But Akinosuke felt such grief at her death that he no longer cared to live.

Now when the legal period of mourning was over, there came to Raishu, from the Tokoyo palace, a *shisha*, or royal messenger. The *shisha* delivered to Akinosuke a message of condolence, and then said to him:

"These are the words which our august master, the King of Tokoyo, commands that I repeat to you: 'We will now send you back to your own people and country. As for the seven children, they are the grandsons and granddaughters of the King, and shall be fitly cared for. Do not, therefore, allow you mind to be troubled concerning them.'"

On receiving this mandate, Akinosuke submissively prepared for his departure. When all his affairs had been settled, and the ceremony of bidding farewell to his counselors and trusted officials had been concluded, he was escorted with much honour to the port. There he embarked upon the ship sent for him; and the ship sailed out into the blue sea, under the blue sky; and the shape of the island of Raishu itself turned blue, and then turned grey, and then vanished forever... And Akinosuke suddenly awoke – under the cedar-tree in his own garden!

For a moment he was stupefied and dazed. But he perceived his two friends still seated near him, drinking and chatting merrily. He stared at them in a bewildered way, and cried aloud,

"How strange!"

"Akinosuke must have been dreaming," one of them exclaimed, with a laugh. "What did you see, Akinosuke, that was strange?"

Then Akinosuke told his dream, that dream of three-and-twenty years' sojourn in the realm of Tokoyo, in the island of Raishu; and they were astonished, because he had really slept for no more than a few minutes.

One *goshi* said:

"Indeed, you saw strange things. We also saw something strange while you were napping. A little yellow butterfly was fluttering over your face for a moment or two; and we watched it. Then it alighted on the ground beside you, close to the tree; and almost as soon as it alighted there, a big, big ant came out of a hole and seized it and pulling it down into the hole. Just before you woke up, we saw that very butterfly come out of the hole again, and flutter over your face as before. And then it suddenly disappeared: we do not know where it went."

"Perhaps it was Akinosuke's soul," the other *goshi* said; "certainly I thought I saw it fly into his mouth... But, even if that butterfly was Akinosuke's soul, the fact would not explain his dream."

"The ants might explain it," returned the first speaker. "Ants are queer beings – possibly goblins... Anyhow, there is a big ant's nest under that cedar-tree."...

"Let us look!" cried Akinosuke, greatly moved by this suggestion. And he went for a spade.

The ground about and beneath the cedar-tree proved to have been excavated, in a most surprising way, by a prodigious colony of ants. The ants had furthermore built inside their excavations; and their tiny constructions of straw, clay, and stems bore an odd resemblance to miniature towns. In the middle of a structure considerably larger than the rest there was a marvelous swarming of small ants around the body of one very big ant, which had yellowish wings and a long black head.

"Why, there is the King of my dream!" cried Akinosuke; "and there is the palace of Tokoyo!... How extraordinary!... Raishu ought to lie somewhere southwest of it – to the left of that big root... Yes! – here it is!... How very strange! Now I am sure that I can find the mountain of Hanryoko, and the grave of the princess..."

In the wreck of the nest he searched and searched, and at last discovered a tiny mound, on the top of which was fixed a water-worn pebble, in shape resembling a Buddhist monument. Underneath it he found – embedded in clay – the dead body of a female ant.

NOTES

1. In Japanese feudal times there was a privileged class of soldier-farmers, free-holders, corresponding to the class of yeomen in

England; and these were called *goshi*.

2. This name "Tokoyo" is indefinite. According to circumstances it may signify any unknown country, or that undiscovered country from which no traveller returns, or that Fairyland of far-eastern fable, the Realm of Horai. The term "Kokuo" means the ruler of a country, therefore a king. The original phrase, *Tokoyo no Kokuo*, might therefore be rendered here as "the Ruler of Horai", or "the King of Fairyland".

RIKI-BAKA

His name was Riki, signifying strength; but the people called him Riki-the-Simple, or Riki-the-Fool – *Riki-Baka* – because he had been born into perpetual childhood. For the same reason they were kind to him, even when he set a house on fire by putting a lighted match to a mosquito-curtain, and clapped his hands for joy to see the blaze. At sixteen years he was a tall, strong lad; but in mind he remained always at the happy age of two, and therefore continued to play with very small children. The bigger children of the neighbourhood, from four to seven years old, did not care to play with him, because he could not learn their songs and games. His favourite toy was a broomstick, which he used as a hobby-horse; and for hours at a time he would ride on that broomstick, up and down the slope in front of my house, with amazing peals of laughter. But at last he became troublesome by reason of his noise; and I had to tell him that he must find another playground. He bowed submissively, and then went off, sorrowfully trailing his broomstick behind him. Gentle at all times, and perfectly harmless if allowed no chance to play with fire, he seldom gave anybody cause for complaint. His relation to the life of our street was scarcely more than that of a dog or a chicken; and when he finally disappeared, I did not miss him. Months and months passed by before anything happened to remind me of Riki.

"What has become of Riki?" I then asked the old woodcutter who supplies our neighbourhood with fuel. I remembered that Riki had often helped him to carry his bundles.

"Riki-Baka?" answered the old man. "Ah, Riki is dead – poor fellow!... Yes, he died nearly a year ago, very suddenly; the doctors said that he had some disease of the brain. And there is a strange story now about that poor Riki.

"When Riki died, his mother wrote his name, 'Riki-Baka', in the palm of his left hand, putting 'Riki' in the Chinese character, and 'Baka' in *kana*[1]. And she repeated many prayers for him, prayers that he might be reborn into some more happy condition.

"Now, about three months ago, in the honourable residence of Nanigashi-Sama, in Kojimachi, a boy was born with characters on the palm of his left hand; and the characters were quite plain to read – *RIKI-BAKA*'!

"So the people of that house knew that the birth must have happened in answer to somebody's prayer; and they caused inquiry to be made everywhere. At least a vegetable-seller brought word to them that there used to be a simple lad, called Riki-Baka, living in the Ushigome quarter, and that he had died during the last autumn; and they sent two men-servants to look for the mother of Riki.

"Those servants found the mother of Riki, and told her what had happened; and she was glad exceedingly – for that Nanigashi house is a very rich and famous house. But the servants said that the family of Nanigashi-Sama were very angry about the word 'Baka' on the child's hand. 'And where is your Riki buried?' the servants asked. 'He is buried in the cemetery of Zendoji,' she told them. 'Please to give us some of the clay of his grave,' they requested.

"So she went with them to the temple Zendoji, and showed them Riki's grave; and they took some of the grave-clay away with them, wrapped up in a *furoshiki*[2].... They gave Riki's mother some money, ten yen."...

"But what did they want with that clay?" I inquired.

"Well," the old man answered, "you know that it would not do to let the child grow up with that name on his hand. And there is no other means of removing characters that come in that way upon the body of a child: *you must rub the skin with clay taken from the grave of the body of the former birth...*"

NOTES

1. *Kana*: the Japanese phonetic alphabet.

2. *Furoshiki*: a square piece of cotton-goods, or other woven material, used as a wrapper in which to carry small packages.

HORAI

Blue vision of depth lost in height, sea and sky interblending through luminous haze. The day is of spring, and the hour morning.

Only sky and sea, one azure enormity... In the fore, ripples are catching a silvery light, and threads of foam are swirling. But a little further off no motion is visible, nor anything save colour: dim warm blue of water widening away to melt into blue of air. Horizon there is none: only distance soaring into space, infinite concavity hollowing before you, and hugely arching above you, the colour deepening with the height. But far in the midway-blue there hangs a faint, faint vision of palace towers, with high roofs horned and curved like moons, some shadowing of splendor strange and old, illumined by a sunshine soft as memory.

...What I have thus been trying to describe is a *kakemono*, that is to say, a Japanese painting on silk, suspended to the wall of my alcove; and the name of it is *Shinkiro*, which signifies "Mirage". But the shapes of the mirage are unmistakable. Those are the glimmering portals of Horai the blest; and those are the moony roofs of the Palace of the Dragon-King; and the fashion of them (though limned by a Japanese brush of today) is the fashion of things Chinese, twenty-one hundred years ago...

Thus much is told of the place in the Chinese books of that time:

In Horai there is neither death nor pain; and there is no winter. The flowers in that place never fade, and the fruits never fail; and if a man taste of those fruits even but once, he can never again feel thirst or hunger. In Horai grow the enchanted plants *so-rin-shi*, and *riku-go-aoi*, and *ban-kon-to*, which heal all manner of sickness; and there grows also the magical grass *yo-shin-shi*, that quickens the dead; and the magical grass is watered by a fairy water of which a single drink confers perpetual youth. The people of Horai eat their rice out of very, very small bowls; but the rice never diminishes within those bowls, however much of it be eaten, until the eater desires no more. And the people of Horai drink their wine out of very, very small cups; but no man can empty one of those cups, however stoutly he may drink, until there comes upon him the pleasant drowsiness of intoxication.

All this and more is told in the legends of the time of the Shin dynasty. But that the people who wrote down those legends ever saw Horai, even in a mirage, is not believable. For really there are no enchanted fruits which leave the eater forever satisfied, nor any magical grass which revives the dead, nor any fountain of fairy water, nor any bowls which never lack rice, nor any cups which never lack wine. It is not true that sorrow and death never enter Horai; neither is it true that there is not any winter. The winter in Horai is cold; and winds then bite to the bone; and the heaping of snow is monstrous on the roofs of the Dragon-King.

Nevertheless there are wonderful things in Horai; and the most wonderful of all has not been mentioned by any Chinese writer. I mean the atmosphere of Horai. It is an atmosphere peculiar to the place; and, because of it, the sunshine in Horai is *whiter* than any other sunshine, a milky light that never dazzles, astonishingly clear, but very soft. This atmosphere is not of our human period: it is enormously old, so old that I feel afraid when I try to think how old it is; and it is not a mixture of nitrogen and oxygen. It is not made of air at all, but of ghost, the substance of quintillions of quintillions of generations of souls blended into one immense translucency, souls of people who thought in ways never resembling our ways. Whatever mortal man inhales that atmosphere, he takes into his blood the thrilling of these spirits; and they change the sense within him, reshaping his notions of Space and Time, so that he can see only as they used to see, and feel only as they used to feel, and think only as they used to think. Soft as sleep are these changes of sense; and Horai, discerned across them, might thus be described:

Because in Horai there is no knowledge of great evil, the hearts of the people never grow old. And, by reason of being always young in heart, the people of Horai smile from birth until death – except when the Gods send sorrow among them; and faces then are veiled until the sorrow goes away. All folk in Horai love and trust each other, as if all were members of a single household; and the speech of the women is like birdsong, because the hearts of them are light as the souls of birds; and the swaying of the sleeves of the maidens at play seems a flutter of wide, soft wings. In Horai nothing is hidden but grief, because there is no reason for shame; and nothing is locked away, because there could not be any theft; and by night as well as by day all doors remain unbarred, because there is no reason for fear. And because the people are fairies – though mortal – all things in Horai, except the Palace of the Dragon-King, are small and quaint and queer; and these fairy-folk do really eat their rice out of very, very small bowls, and drink their wine out of very, very small cups...

Much of this seeming would be due to the inhalation of that ghostly atmosphere – but not all. For the spell wrought by the dead is only the charm of an Ideal, the glamour of an ancient hope; and something of that hope has found fulfillment in many hearts, in the simple beauty of unselfish lives, in the sweetness of Woman...

Evil winds from the West are blowing over Horai; and the magical atmosphere, alas! is shrinking away before them. It lingers now in patches only, and bands, like those long bright bands of cloud that train across the landscapes of Japanese painters. Under these shreds of the elfish vapor you still can find Horai – but not everywhere... Remember that Horai is also called *Shinkiro*, which signifies Mirage, the Vision of the Intangible. And the Vision is fading, never again to appear save in pictures and poems and dreams...

THE LEGEND OF YUREI-DAKI

Near the village of Kurosaka, in the province of Hoki, there is a waterfall called Yurei-Daki, or *The Cascade of Ghosts*. Why it is so called I do not know. Near the foot of the fall there is a small Shinto shrine of the god of the locality, whom the people name Taki-Daimyojin; and in front of the shrine is a little wooden money-box – *saisen-bako* – to receive the offerings of believers. And there is a story about that money-box.

One icy winter's evening, thirty-five years ago, the women and girls employed at a certain *asa-toriba*, or hemp-factory, in Kurosaka, gathered around the big brazier in the spinning-room after their day's work had been done. Then they amused themselves by telling ghost-stories. By the time that a dozen stories had been told, most of the gathering felt uncomfortable; and a girl cried out, just to heighten the pleasure of fear, "Only think of going this night, all by one's self, to the Yurei-Daki!" The suggestion provoked a general scream, followed by nervous bursts of laughter...

"I'll give all the hemp I spun today," mockingly said one of the party, "to the person who goes!"

"So will I," exclaimed another.

"And I," said a third.

"All of us," affirmed a fourth... Then from among the spinners stood up one Yasumoto O-Katsu, the wife of a carpenter; she had her only son, a boy of two years old, snugly wrapped up and asleep upon her back. "Listen," said O-Katsu; "if you will all really agree to make over to me all the hemp spun today, I will go to the Yurei-Daki."

Her proposal was received with cries of astonishment and of defiance. But after having been several times repeated, it was seriously taken. Each of the spinners in turn agreed to give up her share of the day's work to O-Katsu, providing that O-Katsu should go to the Yurei-Daki. "But how are we to know if she really goes there?" a sharp voice asked. "Why, let her bring back the money-box of the god," answered an old woman whom the spinners called Obaa-San, the Grandmother; "that will be proof enough."

"I'll bring it," cried O-Katsu. And out she darted into the street, with her sleeping boy upon her back.

The night was frosty, but clear. Down the empty street O-Katsu hurried; and she saw that all the house fronts were tightly closed, because of the piercing cold. Out of the village, and along the high road she ran – *pichà-pichà* – with the great silence of frozen rice-fields on either hand, and only the stars to light her. Half an hour she followed the open road; then she turned down a narrower way, winding under cliffs. Darker and rougher the path became as she proceeded; but she knew it well, and she soon heard the dull roar of the water. A few minutes more, and the way widened into a glen, and the dull roar suddenly became a loud clamour, and before her she saw, looming against a mass of blackness, the long glimmering of the fall. Dimly she perceived the shrine, the money-box. She rushed forward, put out her hand. .

"*Oi!* O-Katsu-San!" suddenly called a warning voice above the crash of the water.

O-Katsu stood motionless, stupefied by terror. "*Oi!* O-Katsu-San!" again pealed the voice, this time with more of menace in its tone. But O-Katsu was really a bold woman. At once recovering from her stupefaction, she snatched up the money-box and ran. She neither heard nor saw anything more to alarm her until she reached the highroad, where she stopped a moment to take breath. Then she ran on steadily – *pichà-pichà* – till she got to Kurosaka, and thumped at the door of the *asa-toriba*.

How the women and the girls cried out as she entered, panting, with the money-box of the god in her hand! Breathlessly they heard her story; sympathetically they screeched when she told them of the Voice that had called her name, twice, out of the haunted water... What a woman! Brave O-Katsu ! – well had she earned the hemp!

"But your boy must be cold, O-Katsu!" cried the Obaa-San, "let us have him here by the fire!"

"He ought to be hungry," exclaimed the mother; "I must give him his milk presently."

"Poor O-Katsu!" said the Obaa-San, helping to remove the wraps in which the boy had been carried, "why, you are all wet behind! Then, with a husky scream, the helper vociferated, "*Ara! It is blood!*"

And out of the wrappings unfastened there fell to

the floor a blood-soaked bundle of baby clothes that left exposed two very small brown feet, and two very small brown hands – nothing more. *The child's head had been torn right off!*

EATER OF DREAMS

Mjika-yo ya!
Baku no yume ku
Hima mo nashi!

["Alas! how short this night of ours! The Baku will not ever have time to eat our dreams!" –Old Japanese lovesong.]

The name of the creature is Baku, or *Shirokinakatsukami*; and its particular function is the eating of Dreams. It is variously represented and described. An ancient book in my possession states that the male Baku has the body of a horse, the face of a lion, the trunk and tusks of an elephant, the forelock of a rhinoceros, the tail of a cow, and the feet of a tiger. The female Baku is said to differ greatly in shape from the male; but the difference is not clearly set forth.

In the time of the old Chinese learning, pictures of the Baku used to be hung up in Japanese houses, such pictures being supposed to exert the same beneficent power as the creature itself. My ancient book contains this legend about the custom:

"In the Shosei-Roku it is declared that Kotei, while hunting on the Eastern coast, once met with a Baku

*having the body of an animal, but speaking like a man.
Kotei said: 'Since the world is quiet and at peace, why
should we still see goblins? If a Baku be needed to
extinguish evil sprites, then it were better to have a
picture of the Baku suspended to the wall of one's house.
Thereafter, even though some evil Wonder should
appear, it could do no harm."*

Then there is given a long list of evil Wonders, and the
signs of their presence:

*"When the Hen lays a soft egg, the demon's name is
TAIFU. When snakes appear entwined together, the
demon's name is JINZU. When dogs go with their ears
turned back, the demon's name is TAIYO. When the Fox
speaks with the voice of a man, the demon's name is
GWAISHU. When blood appears on the clothes of men,
the demon's name is YUKI. When the rice-pot speaks
with a human voice, the demon's name is KANJO. When
the dream of the night is an evil dream, the demon's
name is RINGETSU..."*

And the old book further observes: *"Whenever any such
evil marvel happens, let the name of the Baku be
invoked: then the evil sprite will immediately sink three
feet under the ground."*

But on the subject of evil Wonders I do not feel
qualified to discourse: it belongs to the unexplored and
appalling world of Chinese demonology, and it has really
very little to do with the subject of the Baku in Japan.

The Japanese Baku is commonly known only as the Eater of Dreams; and the most remarkable fact in relation to the cult of the creature is that the Chinese character representing its name used to be put in gold upon the lacquered wooden pillows of lords and princes. By the virtue and power of this character on the pillow, the sleeper was thought to be protected from evil dreams. It is rather difficult to find such a pillow today: even pictures of the Baku (or *"Hakutaku"*, as it is sometimes called) have become very rare. But the old invocation to the Baku still survives in common parlance: *Baku kurae! Baku kurae!* – "Devour, O Baku! devour my evil dream!" ...When you awake from a nightmare, or from any unlucky dream, you should quickly repeat that invocation three times; then the Baku will eat the dream, and will change the misfortune or the fear into good fortune and gladness.

It was on a very sultry night, during the Period of Greatest Heat, that I last saw the Baku. I had just awakened out of misery; and the hour was the Hour of the Ox; and the Baku came in through the window to ask, "Have you anything for me to eat?"

I gratefully made answer:

"Assuredly! ...Listen, good Baku, to this dream of mine!:

"I was standing in some great white-walled room, where lamps were burning; but I cast no shadow on the naked floor of that room, and there, upon an iron bed, I saw my own dead body. How I had come to die, and when I had died, I could not remember. Women were sitting near the bed, six or seven, and I did not know any of them. They were neither young nor old, and all were dressed in black: watchers I took them to be. They sat motionless and silent: there was no sound in the place; and I somehow felt that the hour was late.

"In the same moment I became aware of something nameless in the atmosphere of the room, a heaviness that weighed upon the will, some viewless numbing power that was slowly growing. Then the watchers began to watch each other, stealthily; and I knew that they were afraid. Soundlessly one rose up, and left the room. Another followed; then another. So, one by one, and lightly as shadows, they all went out. I was left alone with the corpse of myself.

"The lamps still burned clearly; but the terror in the air was thickening. The watchers had stolen away almost as soon as they began to feel it. But I believed that there was yet time to escape; I thought that I could safely delay a moment longer. A monstrous curiosity obliged me to remain: I wanted to look at my own body, to examine it closely... I approached it. I observed it. And I wondered, because it seemed to me very long – unnaturally long...

"Then I thought that I saw one eyelid quiver. But the appearance of motion might have been caused by the trembling of a lamp-flame. I stooped to look – slowly, and very cautiously, because I was afraid that the eyes might open.

"'It is Myself,' I thought, as I bent down, 'and

yet, it is growing queer!' ...The face appeared to be lengthening... 'It is *not* Myself,' I thought again, as I stooped still lower, 'and yet, it cannot be any other!' And I became much more afraid, unspeakably afraid, that the eyes would open...

"*They OPENED!* – horribly they opened! – and that thing sprang, sprang from the bed at me, and fastened upon me, moaning, and gnawing, and rending! Oh! with what madness of terror did I strive against it! But the eyes of it, and the moans of it, and the touch of it, sickened; and all my being seemed about to burst asunder in frenzy of loathing, when – I knew not how I found in my hand an axe. And I struck with the axe – I clove, I crushed, I brayed the Moaner – until there lay before me only a shapeless, hideous, reeking mass – *the abominable ruin of Myself...*

"*Baku kurae! Baku kurae! Baku kurae!* Devour, O Baku! Devour the dream!"

"Nay!" made answer the Baku. "I never eat lucky dreams. That is a very lucky dream – a most fortunate dream... The axe – yes! the Axe of the Excellent Law, by which the monster of Self is utterly destroyed! The best kind of a dream! My friend, I believe in the teaching of the Buddha."

And the Baku went out of the window. I looked after him; and I beheld him fleeing over the miles of moonlit roofs, passing, from house-top to house-top, with amazing soundless leaps, like a great cat...

IN A CUP OF TEA

Have you ever attempted to mount some old tower stairway, spiring up through darkness, and in the heart of that darkness found yourself at the cobwebbed edge of nothing? Or have you followed some coast path, cut along the face of a cliff, only to discover yourself, at a turn, on the jagged verge of a break? The emotional worth of such experience – from a literary point of view – is proved by the force of the sensations aroused, and by the vividness with which they are remembered.

Now there have been curiously preserved, in old Japanese story-books, certain fragments of fiction that produce an almost similar emotional experience.

Perhaps the writer was lazy; perhaps he had a quarrel with the publisher; perhaps he was suddenly called away from his little table, and never came back; perhaps death stopped the writing-brush in the very middle of a sentence.

But no mortal man can ever tell us exactly why these things were left unfinished... I select a typical example.

On the fourth day of the first month of the third Tenwa – that is to say, about two hundred and twenty years ago – the lord Nakagawa Sado, while on his way to make a New Year's visit, halted with his train at a tea-house in

Hakusan, in the Hongo district of Edo. While the party were resting there, one of the lord's armed attendants – a *wakato* ["armed attendant"] named Sekinai – feeling very thirsty, filled for himself a large water-cup with tea. He was raising the cup to his lips when he suddenly perceived, in the transparent yellow infusion, the image or reflection of a face that was not his own. Startled, he looked around, but could see no one near him. The face in the tea appeared, from the coiffure, to be the face of a young *samurai*: it was strangely distinct, and very handsome – delicate as the face of a girl. And it seemed the reflection of a *living* face; for the eyes and the lips were moving. Bewildered by this mysterious apparition, Sekinai threw away the tea, and carefully examined the cup. It proved to be a very cheap water-cup, with no artistic devices of any sort. He found and filled another cup; and again the face appeared in the tea. He then ordered fresh tea, and refilled the cup; and once more the strange face appeared, – this time with a mocking smile. But Sekinai did not allow himself to be frightened. "Whoever you are," he muttered, "you shall delude me no further" – then he swallowed the tea, face and all, and went his way, wondering whether he had swallowed a ghost.

Late in the evening of the same day, while on watch in the palace of the lord Nakagawa, Sekinai was surprised by the soundless coming of a stranger into the apartment. This stranger, a richly dressed young *samurai*, seated himself directly in front of Sekinai, and, saluting the *wakato* with a slight bow, observed:

"I am Shikibu Heinai – I met you today for the first time... You do not seem to recognize me."

He spoke in a very low, but penetrating voice. And Sekinai was astonished to find before him the same sinister, handsome face of which he had seen, and swallowed, the apparition in a cup of tea. It was smiling now, as the phantom had smiled; but the steady gaze of the eyes, above the smiling lips, was at once a challenge and an insult.

"No, I do not recognize you," returned Sekinai, angry but cool; "and perhaps you will now be good enough to inform me how you obtained admission to this house?"

[In feudal times the residence of a lord was strictly guarded at all hours; and no one could enter unannounced, except through some unpardonable negligence on the part of the armed watch.]

"Ah, you do not recognize me!" exclaimed the visitor, in a tone of irony, drawing a little nearer as he spoke. "No, you do not recognize me! Yet you took upon yourself this morning to do me a deadly injury!..."

Sekinai instantly seized the *tanto*[1] at his girdle, and made a fierce thrust at the throat of the man. But the blade seemed to touch no substance. Simultaneously and soundlessly the intruder leaped sideward to the chamber-wall, *and through it!*

The wall showed no trace of his exit. He had traversed it only as the light of a candle passes through lantern-paper.

When Sekinai made report of the incident, his recital astonished and puzzled the retainers. No stranger had been seen either to enter or to leave the palace at the hour of the occurrence; and no one in the service of the lord Nakagawa had ever heard of the name "Shikibu Heinai".

On the following night Sekinai was off duty, and remained at home with his parents. At a rather late hour he was informed that some strangers had called at the house, and desired to speak with him for a moment. Taking his sword, he went to the entrance, and there found three armed men, apparently retainers, waiting in front of the doorstep. The three bowed respectfully to Sekinai; and one of them said:

"Our names are Matsuoka Bungo, Tsuchibashi Bungo, and Okamura Heiroku. We are retainers of the noble Shikibu Heinai. When our master last night deigned to pay you a visit, you struck him with a sword. He was much hurt, and has been obliged to go to the hot springs, where his wound is now being treated. But on the sixteenth day of the coming month he will return; and he will then repay you for the injury done him..."

Without waiting to hear more, Sekinai leaped out, sword in hand, and slashed right and left, at the strangers. But the three men sprang to the wall of the adjoining building, and flitted up the wall like shadows, and...

[Here the old narrative breaks off; the rest of the story exists only in some brain that has been dust for a century. I am able to postulate several possible endings; but none of them would satisfy an Occidental imagination. I prefer to let the reader attempt to decide for himself the probable consequence of swallowing a Soul.]

NOTES

1. *Tanto*: the shorter of the two swords carried by *samurai*. The longer sword was called a *katana*.

COMMON SENSE

Once there lived upon the mountain called Atagoyama, near Kyoto, a certain learned priest who devoted all his time to meditation and the study of the sacred books. The little temple in which he dwelt was far from any village; and he could not, in such a solitude, have obtained without help the common necessaries of life. But several devout country people regularly contributed to his maintenance, bringing him each month supplies of vegetables and of rice.

Among these good folk there was a certain hunter, who sometimes visited the mountain in search of game. One day, when this hunter had brought a bag of rice to the temple, the priest said to him:

"Friend, I must tell you that wonderful things have happened here since the last time I saw you. I do not certainly know why such things should have happened in my unworthy presence. But you are aware that I have been meditating, and reciting the sutras daily, for many years; and it is possible that what has been vouchsafed me is due to the merit obtained through these religious exercises. I am not sure of this. But I am sure that Fugen Bosatsu[1] comes nightly to this temple, riding upon his elephant... Stay here with me this night, friend; then you will be able to see and to worship the Buddha."

"To witness so holy a vision," the hunter replied, "were a privilege indeed! Most gladly I shall stay, and worship with you."

So the hunter remained at the temple. But while the priest was engaged in his religious exercises, the hunter began to think about the promised miracle, and to doubt whether such a thing could be. And the more he thought, the more he doubted. There was a little boy in the temple, an acolyte, and the hunter found an opportunity to question the boy.

"The priest told me," said the hunter, "that Fugen Bosatsu comes to this temple every night. Have you also seen Fugen Bosatsu?"

"Six times, already," the acolyte replied, "I have seen and reverently worshipped Fugen Bosatsu."

This declaration only served to increase the hunter's suspicions, though he did not in the least doubt the truthfulness of the boy. He reflected, however, that he would probably be able to see whatever the boy had seen; and he waited with eagerness for the hour of the promised vision.

Shortly before midnight the priest announced that it was time to prepare for the coming of Fugen Bosatsu. The doors of the little temple were thrown open; and the priest knelt down at the threshold, with his face to the east. The acolyte knelt at his left hand, and the hunter respectfully placed himself behind the priest.

It was the night of the twentieth of the ninth month – a dreary, dark, and very windy night; and the three waited a long time for the coming of Fugen

Bosatsu. But at last a point of white light appeared, like a star, in the direction of the east; and this light approached quickly, growing larger and larger as it came, and illuminating all the slope of the mountain. Presently the light took shape – the shape of a being divine, riding upon a snow-white elephant with six tusks. And, in another moment, the elephant with its shining rider arrived before the temple, and there stood towering, like a mountain of moonlight, wonderful and weird.

Then the priest and the boy, prostrating themselves, began with exceeding fervour to repeat the holy invocation to Fugen Bosatsu. But suddenly the hunter rose up behind them, bow in hand; and, bending his bow to the full, he sent a long arrow whizzing straight at the luminous Buddha, into whose breast it sank up to the very feathers.

Immediately, with a sound like a thunder-clap, the white light vanished, and the vision disappeared. Before the temple there was nothing but windy darkness.

"O miserable man!" cried out the priest, with tears of shame and despair, "O most wretched and wicked man! what have you done ? – what have you done?"

But the hunter received the reproaches of the priest without any sign of compunction or of anger. Then he said, very gently:

"Reverend sir, please try to calm yourself, and listen to me. You thought that you were able to see Fugen

Bosatsu because of some merit obtained through your constant meditations and your recitation of the sutras. But if that had been the case, the Buddha would have appeared to you only – not to me, nor even to the boy. I am an ignorant hunter, and my occupation is to kill; and the taking of life is hateful to the Buddhas. How then should I be able to see Fugen Bosatsu? I have been taught that the Buddhas are everywhere about us, and that we remain unable to see them because of our ignorance and, our imperfections. You – being a learned priest of pure life – might indeed acquire such enlightenment as would enable you to see the Buddhas; but how should a man who kills animals for his livelihood find the power to see the divine? Both I and this little boy could see all that you saw. And let me now assure you, reverend sir, that what you saw was not Fugen Bosatsu, but a goblinry intended to deceive you – perhaps even to destroy you. I beg that you will try to control your feelings until daybreak. Then I will prove to you the truth of what I have said."

At sunrise the hunter and the priest examined the spot where the vision had been standing, and they discovered a thin trail of blood. And after having followed this trail to a hollow some hundred paces away, they came upon the body of a great badger, transfixed by the hunter's arrow.

The priest, although a learned and pious person, had easily been deceived by a *mujina*. But the hunter, an ignorant and irreligious man, was gifted with strong common sense; and by native wit alone he was able at once to detect and to destroy a dangerous a illusion.

NOTES

1. Samantabhadra Bodhisattva, Protector of Buddhism, God of Praxis, in Japanese Buddhism.

IKIRYO

Formerly, in the quarter of Reiganjima, in Edo, there was a great porcelain shop called the Setomonodana, kept by a rich man named Kihei. Kihei had in his employ, for many years, a head clerk named Rokubei. Under Rokubei's care the business prospered; and at last it grew so large that Rokubei found himself unable to manage it without help. He therefore asked and obtained permission to hire an experienced assistant; and he then engaged one of his own nephews, a young man about twenty-two years old, who had learned the porcelain trade in Osaka.

The nephew proved a very capable assistant, shrewder in business than his experienced uncle. His enterprise extended the trade of the house, and Kihei was greatly pleased. But about seven months after his engagement, the young man became very ill, and seemed likely to die. The best physicians in Edo were summoned to attend him; but none of them could understand the nature of his sickness. They prescribed no medicine, and expressed the opinion that such a sickness could only have been caused by some secret grief.

Rokubei imagined that it might be a case of lovesickness. He therefore said to his nephew:

"I have been thinking that, as you are still very young, you might have formed some secret attachment which is making you unhappy, perhaps even making you ill. If this be the truth, you certainly ought to tell me all about your troubles. Here I stand to you in the place of a father, as you are far away from your parents; and if you have any anxiety or sorrow, I am ready to do for you whatever a father should do. If money can help you, do not be ashamed to tell me, even though the amount be large. I think that I could assist you; and I am sure that Kihei would be glad to do anything to make you happy and well."

The sick youth appeared to be embarrassed by these kindly assurances; and for some little time he remained silent. At last he answered:

"Never in this world can I forget those generous words. But I have no secret attachment – no longing for any woman. This sickness of mine is not a sickness that doctors can cure; and money could not help me in the least. The truth is, that I have been so persecuted in this house that I scarcely care to live. Everywhere – by day and by night, whether in the shop or in my room, whether alone or in company – I have been unceasingly followed and tormented by the Shadow of a woman. And it is long, long since I have been able to get even one night's rest. For so soon as I close my eyes, the Shadow of the woman takes me by the throat and strives to strangle me. So I cannot sleep..."

"And why did you not tell me this before?" asked Rokubei.

"Because I thought," the nephew answered, "that it would be of no use to tell you. The Shadow is not the ghost of a dead person. It is made by the hatred of a living person – a person whom you very well know."

"What person?" questioned Rokubei, in great astonishment.

"The mistress of this house," whispered the youth, "the wife of Kihei Sama... She wishes to kill me."

Rokubei was bewildered by this confession. He doubted nothing of what his nephew had said; but he could not imagine a reason for the haunting. An *ikiryo* might be caused by disappointed love, or by violent hate, without the knowledge of the person from whom it had emanated. To suppose any love in this case was impossible; the wife of Kihei was considerably more than fifty years of age. But, on the other hand, what could the young clerk have done to provoke hatred, a hatred capable of producing an *ikiryo*? He had been irreproachably well conducted, unfailingly courteous, and earnestly devoted to his duties. The mystery troubled Rokubei; but, after careful reflection, he decided to tell everything to Kihei, and to request an investigation.

Kihei was astounded; but in the time of forty years he had never had the least reason to doubt the word of Rokubei. He therefore summoned his wife at once, and carefully questioned her, telling her, at the same time, what the sick clerk had said. At first she turned pale, and wept; but, after some hesitation, she answered frankly:

"I suppose that what the new clerk has said about the *ikiryo* is true, though I really tried never to betray, by word or look, the dislike which I could not help feeling for him. You know that he is very skilful in commerce, very shrewd in everything that he does. And you have given him much authority in this house – power over the apprentices and the servants. But our only son, who should inherit this business, is very simple-hearted and easily deceived; and I have long been thinking that your clever new clerk might so delude our boy as to get possession of all this property. Indeed, I am certain that your clerk could at any time, without the least difficulty, and without the least risk to himself, ruin our business and ruin our son. And with this certainty in my mind, I cannot help fearing and hating the man. I have often and often wished that he were dead; I have even wished that it were in my own power to kill him... Yes, I know that it is wrong to hate any one in such a way; but I could not check the feeling. Night and day I have been wishing evil to that clerk. So I cannot doubt that he has really seen the thing of which he spoke to Rokubei."

"How absurd of you," exclaimed Kihei, "to torment yourself thus! Up to the present time that clerk has done no single thing for which he could be blamed; and you have caused him to suffer cruelly... Now if I should send him away, with his uncle, to another town, to establish a branch business, could you not endeavour to think more kindly of him?"

"If I do not see his face or hear his voice," the wife answered, "if you will only send him away from this house, then I think that I shall be able to conquer my hatred of him."

"Try to do so," said Kihei ; "for, if you continue to hate him as you have been hating him, he will certainly die, and you will then be guilty of having caused the death of a man who has done us nothing but good. He has been, in every way, a most excellent servant."

Then Kihei quickly made arrangements for the establishment of a branch house in another city; and he sent Rokubei there with the clerk, to take charge. And thereafter the *ikiryo* ceased to torment the young man, who soon recovered his health.

SHIRYO

On the death of Nomoto Yajiyemon, a *daikwan* [district governor] in the province of Echizen, his clerks entered into a conspiracy to defraud the family of their late master. Under pretext of paying some of the *daikwan*'s debts, they took possession of all the money, valuables, and furniture in his house; and they furthermore prepared a false report to make it appear that he had unlawfully contracted obligations exceeding the worth of his estate. This false report they sent to the Saisho [high official of the Shogunate] and the Saisho thereupon issued a decree banishing the widow and the children of Nomoto from the province of Echizen. For in those times the family of a *daikwan* were held in part responsible, even after his death, for any malfeasance proved against him.

But at the moment when the order of banishment was officially announced to the widow of Nomoto, a strange thing happened to a maidservant in the house. She was seized with convulsions and shudderings, like a person possessed; and when the convulsions passed, she rose up, and cried out to the officers of the Saisho, and to the clerks of her late master:

"Now listen to me! It is not a girl who is speaking to you; it is I, Yajiyemon, Nomoto Yajiyemon, returned to you from the dead. In grief and great anger do I return

– grief and anger caused me by those in whom I vainly put my trust! O you infamous and ungrateful clerks! How could you so forget the favours bestowed upon you, as thus to ruin my property, and to disgrace my name? Here, now, in my presence, let the accounts of my office and of my house be made; and let a servant be sent for the books of the Metsuke [government accountant], so that the estimates may be compared!"

As the maid uttered these words, all present were filled with astonishment; for her voice and her manner were the voice and the manner of Nomoto Yajiyemon. The guilty clerks turned pale. But the representatives of the Saisho at once commanded that the desire expressed by the girl should be fully granted. All the account-books of the office were promptly placed before her, and the books of the Metsuke were brought in; and she began the reckoning. Without making a single error, she went through all the accounts, writing down the totals and correcting every false entry. And her writing, as she wrote, was seen to be the very writing of Nomoto Yajiyemon.

Now this reexamination of the accounts not only proved that there had been no indebtedness, but also showed that there had been a surplus in the office treasury at the time of the *daikwan*'s death. Thus the villany of the clerks became manifest.

And when all the accounts had been made up, the girl said, speaking in the very voice of Nomoto Yajiyemon:

"Now everything is finished; and I can do

nothing further in the matter. So I shall go back to the place from which I came." Then she lay down, and instantly fell asleep; and she slept like a dead person during two days and two nights. [For great weariness and deep sleep fall upon the possessed, when the possessing spirit passes from them.] When she again awoke, her voice and her manner were the voice and the manner of a young girl; and neither at that time, nor at any time after, could she remember what had happened while she was possessed by the ghost of Nomoto Yajiyemon.

A report of this event was promptly sent to the Saisho; and the Saisho, in consequence, not only revoked the order of banishment, but made large gifts to the family of the *daikwan*. Later on, various posthumous honours were conferred upon Nomoto Yajiyemon; and for many subsequent years his house was favoured by the Government, so that it prospered greatly. But the clerks received the punishment they deserved.

THE STORY OF O-KAME

O-Kame, daughter of the rich Gonyemon of Nagoshi, in the province of Tosa, was very fond of her husband, Hachiyemon. She was twenty-two, and Hachiyemon twenty-five. She was so fond of him that people imagined her to be jealous. But he never gave her the least cause for jealousy; and it is certain that no single unkind word was ever spoken between them.

Unfortunately the health of O-Kame was feeble. Within less than two years after her marriage she was attacked by a disease, then prevalent in Tosa, and the best doctors were not able to cure her. Persons seized by this malady could not eat or drink; they remained constantly drowsy and languid, and troubled by strange fancies. And, in spite of constant care, O-Kame grew weaker and weaker, day by day, until it became evident, even to herself, that she was going to die.

Then she called her husband, and said to him:

"I cannot tell you how good you have been to me during this miserable sickness of mine. Surely no one could have been more kind. But that only makes it all the harder for me to leave you now... Think! I am not yet even twenty-five, and I have the best husband in all this world, and yet I must die!... Oh, no, no! it is useless to talk to me about hope; the best Chinese doctors could do nothing for me. I did think to live a few months longer;

but when I saw my face this morning in the mirror, I knew that I must die today – yes, this very day. And there is something that I want to beg you to do for me, if you wish me to die quite happy."

"Only tell me what it is," Hachiyemon answered; "and if it be in my power to do, I shall be more than glad to do it."

"No, no – you will not be glad to do it," she returned; "you are still so young! It is difficult – very, very difficult – even to ask you to do such a thing; yet the wish for it is like a fire burning in my breast. I must speak it before I die... My dear, you know that sooner or later, after I am dead, they will want you to take another wife. Will you promise me – can you promise me – not to marry again?"

"Only that!" Hachiyemon exclaimed. "Why, if that be all that you wanted to ask for, your wish is very easily granted. With all my heart I promise you that no one shall ever take your place."

"*Aa! Urêshiya!*" cried O-Kame, half-rising from her couch; "oh, how happy you have made me!"

And she fell back dead.

Now the health of Hachiyemon appeared to fail after the death of O-Kame. At first the change in his aspect was attributed to natural grief, and the villagers only said, "How fond of her he must have been!" But, as the months went by, he grew paler and weaker, until at last he became so thin and wan that he looked more like a ghost than a man. Then people began to suspect that sorrow alone could not explain this sudden decline of a man so young. The doctors said that Hachiyemon was not suffering from any known form of disease: they could not account for his condition; but they suggested that it might have been caused by some very unusual trouble of mind. Hachiyemon's parents questioned him in vain; he had no cause for sorrow, he said, other than what they already knew. They counselled him to remarry; but he protested that nothing could ever induce him to break his promise to the dead.

Thereafter Hachiyemon continued to grow visibly weaker, day by day; and his family despaired of his life. But one day his mother, who felt sure that he had been concealing something from her, adjured him so earnestly to tell her the real cause of his decline, and wept so bitterly before him, that he was not able to resist her entreaties.

"Mother," he said, "it is very difficult to speak about this matter, either to you or to any one; and, perhaps, when I have told you everything, you will not be able to believe me. But the truth is that O-Kame can find no rest in the other world, and that the Buddhist services repeated for her have been said in vain. Perhaps she will never be able to rest unless I go with her on the long black journey. For every night she returns, and lies down by my side. Every night, since the day of her funeral, she has come back. And sometimes I doubt if she be really dead; for she looks and acts just as when she lived, except that she talks to me only in whispers. And she always bids me tell no one that she comes. It may be that she wants me to die; and I should not care to live for my own sake only. But it is true, as you have said, that my body really belongs to my parents, and that I owe to them the first duty. So now, mother, I tell you the whole truth... Yes: every night she comes, just as I am about to sleep; and she remains until dawn. As soon as she hears the temple-bell, she goes away."

When the mother of Hachiyemon had heard these things, she was greatly alarmed; and, hastening at once to the parish-temple, she told the priest all that her son had confessed, and begged for ghostly help. The priest, who was a man of great age and experience, listened without surprise to the recital, and then said to her:

"It is not the first time that I have known such a thing to happen; and I think that I shall be able to save your son. But he is really in great danger. I have seen the shadow of death upon his face; and, if O-Kame returns but once again, he will never behold another sunrise. Whatever can be done or him must be done quickly. Say nothing of the matter to your son but assemble the members of both families as soon as possible, and tell them to come to the temple without delay. For your son's sake it will be necessary to open the grave of O-Kame."

So the relatives assembled at the temple; and when the priest had obtained their consent to the opening of the sepulchre, he led the way to the cemetery. Then, under his direction, the tombstone of O-Kame was shifted, the grave opened, and the coffin raised. And when the coffin-lid had been removed, all present were startled; for O-Kame sat before them with a smile upon her face, seeming as comely as before the time of her sickness; and there was not any sign of death upon her. But when the priest told his assistants to lift the dead woman out of the coffin, the astonishment changed to fear; for the corpse was blood-warm to the touch, and still flexible as in life, notwithstanding the squatting posture in which it had remained so long.[1]

It was borne to the mortuary chapel; and there the priest, with a writing-brush, traced upon the brow and breast and limbs of the body the Sanscrit characters (*bonji*) of certain holy talismanic words. And he performed a *Segaki*-service for the spirit of O-Kame, before suffering her corpse to be restored to the ground. She never again visited her husband; and Hachiyemon gradually recovered his health and strength. But whether he always kept his promise, the Japanese story-teller does not say.

NOTES

1. The Japanese dead are placed in a sitting posture in the coffin, which is almost square in form.

THE STORY OF CHUGORO

A long time ago there lived, in the Koishikawa quarter of
Edo, a *hatamoto*[1] named Suzuki, whose *yashiki* was
situated on the bank of the Yedogawa, not far from the
bridge called Naka-no-hashi. And among the retainers of
this Suzuki there was an *ashigaru*[2] named Chugoro.
Chugoro was a handsome lad, very amiable and clever,
and much liked by his comrades.

For several years Chugoro remained in the
service of Suzuki, conducting himself so well that no fault
was found with him. But at last the other *ashigaru*
discovered that Chugoro was in the habit of leaving the
yashiki every night, by way of the garden, and staying
out until a little before dawn. At first they said nothing to
him about this strange behaviour; for his absences did
not interfere with any regular duty, and were supposed
to be caused by some love-affair. But after a time he
began to look pale and weak; and his comrades,
suspecting some serious folly, decided to interfere.
Therefore, one evening, just as he was about to steal
away from the house, an elderly retainer called him
aside, and said:

"Chugoro, my lad, we know that you go out every
night and stay away until early morning; and we have
observed that you are looking unwell. We fear that you
are keeping bad company, and injuring your health. And

159

unless you can give a good reason for your conduct, we shall think that it is our duty to report this matter to the Chief Officer. In any case, since we are your comrades and friends, it is but right that we should know why you go out at night, contrary to the custom of this house."

Chugoro appeared to be very much embarrassed and alarmed by these words. But after a short silence he passed into the garden, followed by his comrade. When the two found themselves well out of hearing of the rest, Chugoro stopped, and said:

"I will now tell you everything; but I must entreat you to keep my secret. If you repeat what I tell you, some great misfortune may befall me.

"It was in the early part of last spring – about five months ago – that I first began to go out at night, on account of a love-affair. One evening, when I was returning to the *yashiki* after a visit to my parents, I saw a woman standing by the riverside, not far from the main gateway. She was dressed like a person of high rank; and I thought it strange that a woman so finely dressed should be standing there alone at such an hour. But I did not think that I had any right to question her; and I was about to pass her by, without speaking, when she stepped forward and pulled me by the sleeve. Then I saw that she was very young and handsome. 'Will you not walk with me as far as the bridge?' she said; 'I have something to tell you.' Her voice was very soft and pleasant; and she smiled as she spoke; and her smile was hard to resist. So I walked with her toward the bridge; and on the way she told me that she had often seen me going in and out of the *yashiki*, and had taken a fancy to me. 'I wish to have you for my husband,' she said; 'if you can like me, we shall be able to make each other very happy.' I did not know how to answer her; but I thought her very charming. As we neared the bridge, she pulled my sleeve again, and led me down the bank to the very edge of the river. 'Come in with me,' she whispered, and pulled me toward the water. It is deep there, as you know; and I became all at once afraid of her, and tried to turn back. She smiled, and caught me by the wrist, and said, 'Oh, you must never be afraid with me!' And, somehow, at the touch of her hand, I became more helpless than a child. I felt like a person in a dream who tries to run, and cannot move hand or foot. Into the deep water she stepped, and drew me with her; and I neither saw nor heard nor felt anything more until I found myself walking beside her through what seemed to be a great palace, full of light. I was neither wet nor cold: everything around me was dry and warm and beautiful. I could not understand where I was, nor how I had come there. The woman led me by the hand: we passed through room after room, through ever so many rooms, all empty, but very fine, until we entered into a guest-room of a thousand mats. Before a great alcove, at the farther end, lights were burning, and cushions laid as for a feast; but I saw no guests. She led me to the place of honour, by the alcove, and seated herself in front of me, and said: 'This is my home: do you think that you could be happy with me here?' As she asked the question she smiled; and I thought that her smile was more beautiful than anything else in the world;

and out of my heart I answered, 'Yes...' In the same moment I remembered the story of Urashima[3]; and I imagined that she might be the daughter of a god; but I feared to ask her any questions... Presently maid-servants came in, bearing rice-wine and many dishes, which they set before us. Then she who sat before me said: 'tonight shall be our bridal night, because you like me; and this is our wedding-feast.' We pledged ourselves to each other for the time of seven existences; and after the banquet we were conducted to a bridal chamber, which had been prepared for us.

"It was yet early in the morning when she awoke me, and said: 'My dear one, you are now indeed my husband. But for reasons which I cannot tell you, and which you must not ask, it is necessary that our marriage remain secret. To keep you here until daybreak would cost both of us our lives. Therefore do not, I beg of you, feel displeased because I must now send you back to the house of your lord. You can come to me tonight again, and every night hereafter, at the same hour that we first met. Wait always for me by the bridge; and you will not have to wait long. But remember, above all things, that our marriage must be a secret, and that, if you talk about it, we shall probably be separated forever.'

"I promised to obey her in all things, remembering the fate of Urashima, and she conducted me through many rooms, all empty and beautiful, to the entrance. There she again took me by the wrist, and everything suddenly became dark, and I knew nothing more until I found myself standing alone on the river bank, close to the Naka-no-hashi. When I got back to the *yashiki*, the temple bells had not yet begun to ring.

"In the evening I went again to the bridge, at the hour she had named, and I found her waiting for me. She took me with her, as before, into the deep water, and into the wonderful place where we had passed our bridal night. And every night, since then, I have met and parted from her in the same way. tonight she will certainly be waiting for me, and I would rather die than disappoint her: therefore I must go... But let me again entreat you, my friend, never to speak to any one about what I have told you."

The elder *ashigaru* was surprised and alarmed by this story. He felt that Chugoro had told him the truth; and the truth suggested unpleasant possibilities. Probably the whole experience was an illusion, and an illusion produced by some evil power for a malevolent end. Nevertheless, if really bewitched, the lad was rather to be pitied than blamed; and any forcible interference would be likely to result in mischief. So the *ashigaru* answered kindly:

I shall never speak of what you have told me – never, at least, while you remain alive and well. Go and meet the woman; but – beware of her! I fear that you are being deceived by some wicked spirit."

Chugoro only smiled at the old man's warning, and hastened away. Several hours later he re-entered the *yashiki*, with a strangely dejected look. "Did you meet her?" whispered his comrade. "No," replied Chugoro; "she was not there. For the first time, she was not there.

I think that she will never meet me again. I did wrong, to tell you; I was very foolish to break my promise..."

The other vainly tried to console him. Chugoro lay down, and spoke no word more. He was trembling from head to foot, as if he had caught a chill.

When the temple bells announced the hour of dawn, Chugoro tried to get up, and fell back senseless. He was evidently sick – deathly sick. A Chinese physician was summoned.

"Why, the man has no blood!" exclaimed the doctor, after a careful examination; "there is nothing but water in his veins! It will be very difficult to save him... What maleficence is this?"

Everything was done that could be done to save Chugoro's life – but in vain. He died as the sun went down. Then his comrade related the whole story.

"Ah! I might have suspected as much!" exclaimed the doctor... "No power could have saved him. He was not the first whom she destroyed."

"Who is she ? – or *what* is she?" the *ashigaru* asked, "A Fox-Woman?"

"No; she has been haunting this river from ancient time. She loves the blood of the young..."

"A Serpent-Woman? A Dragon-Woman?"

"No, no! If you were to see her under that bridge by moonlight, she would appear to you a very loathsome creature."

"But what kind of a creature?"

"Simply, a frog – *a great, ugly frog!*"

NOTES

1. *Hatamoto*: a direct retainer of the Shogun.

2. A*shigaru*: the lowest class of retainers in military service.

3. A popular legend of the sea: Urashima Taro was a Japanese fisherman who rescued a turtle and was rewarded for this with a visit to Ryugu, the palace of Ryujin, the Dragon God, under the sea. He stayed there for three days but, upon his return to his village, found himself 300 years in the future.

THE RECONCILIATION

There was a young *samurai* of Kyōto who had been reduced to poverty by the ruin of his lord, and found himself obliged to leave his home, and to take service with the Governor of a distant province. Before quitting the capital, this *samurai* divorced his wife, a good and beautiful woman, under the belief that he could better obtain promotion by another alliance. He then married the daughter of a family of some distinction, and took her with him to the district whither he had been called.

But it was in the time of the thoughtlessness of youth, and the sharp experience of want, that the *samurai* could not understand the worth of the affection so lightly cast away. His second marriage did not prove a happy one; the character of his new wife was hard and selfish; and he soon found every cause to think with regret of Kyoto days. Then he discovered that he still loved his first wife – loved her more than he could ever love the second; and he began to feel how unjust and how thankless he had been. Gradually his repentance deepened into a remorse that left him no peace of mind. Memories of the woman he had wronged – her gentle speech, her smiles, her dainty, pretty ways, her faultless patience – continually haunted him. Sometimes in dreams he saw her at her loom, weaving as when she toiled night and day to help him during the years of their distress: more often he saw her kneeling alone in the desolate little room where he had left her, veiling her tears with her poor worn sleeve. Even in the hours of official duty, his thoughts would wander back to her: then he would ask himself how she was living, what she was doing. Something in his heart assured him that she could not accept another husband, and that she never would refuse to pardon him. And he secretly resolved to seek her out as soon as he could return to Kyoto, then to beg her forgiveness, to take her back, to do everything that a man could do to make atonement. But the years went by.

At last the Governor's official term expired, and the *samurai* was free. "Now I will go back to my dear one," he vowed to himself. "Ah, what a cruelty, what a folly to have divorced her!" He sent his second wife to her own people (she had given him no children); and hurrying to Kyoto, he went at once to seek his former companion, not allowing himself even the time to change his travelling-garb.

When he reached the street where she used to live, it was late in the night, the night of the tenth day of the ninth month; and the city was silent as a cemetery. But a bright moon made everything visible; and he found the house without difficulty. It had a deserted look: tall weeds were growing on the roof. He knocked at the sliding-doors, and no one answered. Then, finding that the doors had not been fastened from within, he pushed them open, and entered. The front room was matless and empty: a chilly wind was blowing through crevices in the planking; and the moon shone through a ragged break in the wall of the alcove. Other rooms presented a like forlorn condition. The house, to all seeming, was unoccupied. Nevertheless, the *samurai* determined to visit one other apartment at the further end of the dwelling, a very small room that had been his wife's favourite resting-place. Approaching the sliding-screen that closed it, he was startled to perceive a glow within. He pushed the screen aside, and uttered a cry of joy; for he saw her there, sewing by the light of a paper-lamp. Her eyes at the same instant met his own; and with a happy smile she greeted him, asking only: "When did you come back to Kyoto? How did you find your way here to me, through all those black rooms?" The years had not changed her. Still she seemed as fair and young as in his fondest memory of her; but sweeter than any memory there came to him the music of her voice, with its trembling of pleased wonder.

Then joyfully he took his place beside her, and told her all: how deeply he repented his selfishness, how wretched he had been without her, how constantly he had regretted her, how long he had hoped and planned to make amends; caressing her the while, and asking her forgiveness over and over again. She answered him, with loving gentleness, according to his heart's desire, entreating him to cease all self-reproach. It was wrong, she said, that he should have allowed himself to suffer on her account: she had always felt that she was not worthy to be his wife. She knew that he had separated from her, notwithstanding, only because of poverty; and while he lived with her, he had always been kind; and she had never ceased to pray for his happiness. But even if there had been a reason for speaking of amends, this honourable visit would be ample amends; what greater happiness than thus to see him again, though it were only for a moment? "Only for a moment!" he answered, with a glad laugh, "say, rather, for the time of seven existences! My loved one, unless you forbid, I am coming back to live with you always – always – always! Nothing shall ever separate us again. Now I have means and friends: we need not fear poverty. tomorrow my goods will be brought here; and my servants will come to wait upon you; and we shall make this house beautiful.... tonight," he added, apologetically, "I came thus late – without even changing my dress – only because of the longing I had to see you, and to tell you this." She seemed greatly pleased by these words; and in her turn she told him about all that had happened in Kyoto since the time of his departure, excepting her own sorrows, of which she sweetly refused to speak. They chatted far into the night: then she conducted him to a warmer room, facing south, a room that had been their bridal chamber in former time. "Have you no one in the house to help you?" he asked, as she began to prepare the couch for him. "No," she answered, laughing cheerfully: "I could not afford a servant; so I have been living all alone." "You will have plenty of servants tomorrow," he said, "good servants, and everything else that you need." They lay down to rest, not to sleep: they had too much to tell each other; and they talked of the past and the present and the future, until the dawn was grey. Then, involuntarily, the *samurai* closed his eyes, and slept.

When he awoke, the daylight was streaming through the chinks of the sliding-shutters; and he found himself, to his utter amazement, lying upon the naked boards of a mouldering floor.... Had he only dreamed a dream? No: she was there; she slept.... He bent above her, and looked, and shrieked; for the sleeper had no face!... Before him, wrapped in its grave-sheet only, lay the corpse of a woman – a corpse so wasted that *little remained save the bones, and the long black tangled hair.*

Slowly, as he stood shuddering and sickening in the sun, the icy horror yielded to a despair so intolerable, a pain so atrocious, that he clutched at the mocking shadow of a doubt. Feigning ignorance of the neighbourhood, he ventured to ask his way to the house in which his wife had lived.

"There is no one in that house," said the person questioned. "It used to belong to the wife of a *samurai* who left the city several years ago. He divorced her in order to marry another woman before he went away; and she fretted a great deal, and so became sick. She had no relatives in Kyoto, and nobody to care for her; and she died in the autumn of the same year, on the tenth day of the ninth month...."

THE SCREEN-MAIDEN

"In Chinese and in Japanese books there are related many stories, both of ancient and of modern times, about pictures that were so beautiful as to exercise a magical influence upon the beholder. And concerning such beautiful pictures, whether pictures of flowers or of birds or of people, painted by famous artists, it is further told that the shapes of the creatures or the persons, therein depicted, would separate themselves from the paper or the silk upon which they had been painted, and would perform various acts; so that they became, by their own will, really alive. We shall not now repeat any of the stories of this class which have been known to everybody from ancient times. But even in modern times the fame of the pictures painted by Hishigawa Kichibei – 'Hishigawa's Portraits' – has become widespread in the land."

–Hakubai-En Rosui[1]

Hakubai-En Rosui relates the following story about one of these so-called portraits:

There was a young scholar of Kyoto whose name was Tokkei. He used to live in the street called Muromachi. One evening, while on his way home after a visit, his attention was attracted by an old single-leaf screen [*tsuitate*], exposed for sale before the shop of a dealer in second-hand goods. It was only a paper-covered screen; but there was painted upon it the full-length figure of a girl which caught the young man's fancy. The price asked was very small: Tokkei bought the screen, and took it home with him.

When he looked again at the screen, in the solitude of his own room, the picture seemed to him much more beautiful than before. Apparently it was a real likeness, the portrait of a girl fifteen or sixteen years old; and every little detail in the painting of the hair, eyes, eyelashes, mouth, had been executed with a delicacy and a truth beyond praise. The *manajiri*[2] seemed "like a lotus-blossom courting favour"; the lips were "like the smile of a red flower"; the whole young face was inexpressibly sweet. If the real girl so portrayed had been equally lovely, no man could have looked upon her without losing his heart. And Tokkei believed that she must have been thus lovely; for the figure seemed alive, ready to reply to anybody who might speak to it.

Gradually, as he continued to gaze at the picture, he felt himself bewitched by the charm of it. "Can there really have been in this world," he murmured to himself, "so delicious a creature? How gladly would I give my life – nay, a thousand years of life! – to hold her in my arms even for a moment!" In short, he became enamoured of the picture, so much enamoured of it as to feel that he never could love any woman except the person whom it represented. Yet that person, if still alive, could no longer resemble the painting: perhaps she had been buried long before he was born!

Day by day, nevertheless, this hopeless passion grew upon him. He could not eat; he could not sleep: neither could he occupy his mind with those studies which had formerly delighted him. He would sit for hours before the picture, talking to it, neglecting or forgetting everything else. And at last he fell sick – so sick that he believed himself going to die.

Now among the friends of Tokkei there was one venerable scholar who knew many strange things about old pictures and about young hearts. This aged scholar, hearing of Tokkei's illness, came to visit him, and saw the screen, and understood what had happened. Then Tokkei, being questioned, confessed everything to his friend, and declared: "If I cannot find such a woman, I shall die."

The old man said:

"That picture was painted by Hishigawa Kichibei – painted from life. The person whom it represented is not now in the world. But it is said that Hishigawa Kichibei painted her mind as well as her form, and that her spirit lives in the picture. So I think that you can win her."

Tokkei half rose from his bed, and stared eagerly at the speaker.

"You must give her a name," the old man continued; "and you must sit before her picture every day, and keep your thoughts constantly fixed upon her, and call her gently by the name which you have given her, *until she answers you...*"

"Answers me!" exclaimed the lover, in breathless amazement.

"Oh, yes," the adviser responded, "she will certainly answer you. But you must be ready, when she answers you, to present her with what I am going to tell you...."

"I will give her my life!" cried Tokkei.

"No," said the old man; "you will present her with a cup of wine that has been bought at one hundred different wine-shops. Then she will come out of the screen to accept the wine. After that, probably she herself will tell you what to do."

With these words the old man went away. His advice aroused Tokkei from despair. At once he seated himself before the picture, and called it by the name of a girl – what name the Japanese narrator has forgotten to tell us – over and over again, very tenderly. That day it made no answer, nor the next day, nor the next. But Tokkei did not lose faith or patience; and after many days it suddenly one evening answered to its name:

"*Hai!*"

Then quickly, quickly, some of the wine from a hundred different wine-shops was poured out, and reverentially presented in a little cup. And the girl stepped from the screen, and walked upon the matting of the room, and knelt to take the cup from Tokkei's hand, asking, with a delicious smile:

"How could you love me so much?"

[Says the Japanese narrator: "She was much

more beautiful than the picture, beautiful to the tips of her finger-nails, beautiful also in heart and temper, lovelier than anybody else in the world." What answer Tokkei made to her question is not recorded: it will have to be imagined.]

"But will you not soon get tired of me?" she asked.

"Never while I live!" he protested.

"And after?" she persisted; for the Japanese bride is not satisfied with love for one life-time only.

"Let us pledge ourselves to each other," he entreated, "for the time of seven existences."

"If you are ever unkind to me," she said, "I will go back to the screen."

They pledged each other. I suppose that Tokkei was a good boy, for his bride never returned to the screen. The space that she had occupied upon it remained a blank.

How very seldom do such things happen in this world!

NOTES

1. Hakubai-En Rosui died in the eighteenth year of Kyoho (1733). The painter to whom he refers – better known to collectors as Hishigawa Kichibei Moronobu – flourished during the latter part of the seventeenth century. Beginning his career as a dyer's apprentice, he won his reputation as an artist about 1680, when he may be said to have founded the *ukiyo-e* school of illustration. Hishigawa was especially a delineator of what are called *furii* ("elegant manners"), the aspects of life among the upper classes of society.

2. Also written *mejiri*, the exterior canthus of the eye. The Japanese

(like the old Greek and the old Arabian poets) have many curious dainty words and similes to express particular beauties of the hair, eyes, eyelids, lips, fingers, etc.

THE CORPSE-RIDER

The body was cold as ice; the heart had long ceased to beat: yet there were no other signs of death. Nobody even spoke of burying the woman. She had died of grief and anger at having been divorced. It would have been useless to bury her, because the last undying wish of a dying person for vengeance can burst asunder any tomb and rift the heaviest graveyard stone. People who lived near the house in which she was lying fled from their homes. They knew that she was only waiting for the return of the man who had divorced her.

At the time of her death he was on a journey. When he came back and was told what had happened, terror seized him. "If I can find no help before dark," he thought to himself, "she will tear me to pieces." It was yet only the Hour of the Dragon;[1] but he knew that he had no time to lose.

He went at once to an *inyoshi*[2] and begged for succor. The *inyoshi* knew the story of the dead woman; and he had seen the body. He said to the supplicant: "A very great danger threatens you. I will try to save you. But you must promise to do whatever I shall tell you to do. There is only one way by which you can be saved. It is a fearful way. But unless you find the courage to attempt it, she will tear you limb from limb. If you can be brave, come to me again in the evening before sunset."

The man shuddered; but he promised to do whatever should be required of him.

At sunset the *inyoshi* went with him to the house where the body was lying. The *inyoshi* pushed open the sliding-doors, and told his client to enter. It was rapidly growing dark. "I dare not!" gasped the man, quaking from head to foot; "I dare not even look at her!" "You will have to do much more than look at her," declared the *inyoshi*; "and you promised to obey. Go in!" He forced the trembler into the house and led him to the side of the corpse.

The dead woman was lying on her face. "Now you must get astride upon her," said the *inyoshi*, "and sit firmly on her back, as if you were riding a horse... Come! – you must do it!" The man shivered so that the *inyoshi* had to support him – shivered horribly; but he obeyed. "Now take her hair in your hands," commanded the *inyoshi*, "half in the right hand, half in the left... So!... You must grip it like a bridle. Twist your hands in it – both hands – tightly. That is the way!... Listen to me! You must stay like that till morning. You will have reason to be afraid in the night – plenty of reason. But whatever may happen, never let go of her hair. If you let go, even for one second, *she will tear you into gobbets!*"

The *inyoshi* then whispered some mysterious words into the ear of the body, and said to its rider: "Now, for my own sake, I must leave you alone with her... Remain as you are!... Above all things, remember that you must not let go of her hair." And he went away, closing the doors behind him.

Hour after hour the man sat upon the corpse in black fear; and the hush of the night deepened and deepened about him till he screamed to break it. Instantly the body sprang beneath him, as to cast him off; and the dead woman cried out loudly, "Oh, how heavy it is! Yet I shall bring that fellow here now!"

Then tall she rose, and leaped to the doors, and flung them open, and rushed into the night, always bearing the weight of the man. But he, shutting his eyes, kept his hands twisted in her long hair, tightly, tightly, though fearing with such a fear that he could not even moan. How far she went, he never knew. He saw nothing: he heard only the sound of her naked feet in the dark – *pichà-pichà, pichà-pichà* – and the hiss of her breathing as she ran.

At last she turned, and ran back into the house, and lay down upon the floor exactly as at first. Under the man she panted and moaned till the cocks began to crow. Thereafter she lay still.

But the man, with chattering teeth, sat upon her until the *inyoshi* came at sunrise. "So you did not let go of her hair!"observed the *inyoshi*, greatly pleased. "That is well ... Now you can stand up." He whispered again into the ear of the corpse, and then said to the man: "You must have passed a fearful night; but nothing else could have saved you. Hereafter you may feel secure from her vengeance."

NOTES

1. *Tatsu-no-koku*, or the Hour of the Dragon, by old Japanese time, began at about eight o'clock in the morning.

2. *Inyoshi*: a professor or master of the science of *in-yo*, the old Chinese nature-philosophy, based upon the theory of a male and a female principle pervading the universe.

THE GRATITUDE OF THE SAMEBITO

There was a man named Tawaraya Totaro, who lived in the Province of Omi. His house was situated on the shore of Lake Biwa, not far from the famous temple called Ishiyamadera. He had some property, and lived in comfort; but at the age of twenty-nine he was still unmarried. His greatest ambition was to marry a very beautiful woman; and he had not been able to find a girl to his liking.

One day, as he was passing over the Long Bridge of Seta, he saw a strange being crouching close to the parapet. The body of this being resembled the body of a man, but was black as ink; its face was like the face of a demon; its eyes were green as emeralds; and its beard was like the beard of a dragon. Totaro was at first very much startled. But the green eyes looked at him so gently that after a moment's hesitation he ventured to question the creature. Then it answered him, saying: "I am a Samebito, a Shark-Man of the sea; and until a short time ago I was in the service of the Eight Great Dragon-Kings [*Hachi-Dai-Ryu-O*] as a subordinate officer in the Dragon-Palace [*Ryugu*].[1] But because of a small fault which I committed, I was dismissed from the Dragon-Palace, and also banished from the Sea. Since then I have been wandering about here, unable to get any food, or even a place to lie down. If you can feel any pity for me, do, I beseech you, help me to find a shelter, and let me have something to eat!"

This petition was uttered in so plaintive a tone, and in so humble a manner, that Totaro's heart was touched. "Come with me," he said. "There is in my garden a large and deep pond where you may live as long as you wish; and I will give you plenty to eat."

The Samebito followed Totaro home, and appeared to be much pleased with the pond.

Thereafter, for nearly half a year, this strange guest dwelt in the pond, and was every day supplied by Totaro with such food as sea-creatures like.

Now, in the seventh month of the same year, there was a female pilgrimage (*nyonin-mode*) to the great Buddhist temple called Miidera, in the neighbouring town of Otsu; and Totaro went to Otsu to attend the festival. Among the multitude of women and young girls there assembled, he observed a person of extraordinary beauty. She seemed about sixteen years old; her face was fair and pure as snow; and the loveliness of her lips assured the beholder that their every utterance would sound "as sweet as the voice of a nightingale singing upon a plum-tree". Totaro fell in love with her at sight. When she left the temple he followed her at a respectful distance, and discovered that she and her mother were staying for a few days at a certain house in the neighbouring village of Seta. By questioning some of the village folk, he was able also to learn that her name was Tamana; that she was unmarried; and that her family appeared to be unwilling that she should marry a man of ordinary rank, for they demanded as a betrothal-gift a casket containing ten thousand jewels.

Totaro returned home very much dismayed by this information. The more that he thought about the strange betrothal-gift demanded by the girl's parents, the more he felt that he could never expect to obtain her for his wife. Even supposing that there were as many as ten thousand jewels in the whole country, only a great prince could hope to procure them.

But not even for a single hour could Totaro banish from his mind the memory of that beautiful being. It haunted him so that he could neither eat nor sleep; and it seemed to become more and more vivid as the days went by. And at last he became ill, so ill that he could not lift his head from the pillow. Then he sent for a doctor.

The doctor, after having made a careful examination, uttered an exclamation of surprise. "Almost any kind of sickness," he said, "can be cured by proper medical treatment, except the sickness of love. Your ailment is evidently love-sickness. There is no cure for it. In ancient times Roya-O Hakuyo died of that sickness; and you must prepare yourself to die as he died." So saying, the doctor went away, without even giving any medicine to Totaro.

About this time the Shark-Man that was living in the garden-pond heard of his master's sickness, and came into the house to wait upon Totaro. And he tended him with the utmost affection both by day and by night. But he did not know either the cause or the serious nature of the sickness until nearly a week later, when

Totaro, thinking himself about to die, uttered these words of farewell:

"I suppose that I have had the pleasure of caring for you thus long, because of some relation that grew up between us in a former state of existence. But now I am very sick indeed, and every day my sickness becomes worse; and my life is like the morning dew which passes away before the setting of the sun. For your sake, therefore, I am troubled in mind. Your existence has depended upon my care; and I fear that there will be no one to care for you and to feed you when I am dead.... My poor friend!... Alas! our hopes and our wishes are always disappointed in this unhappy world!"

No sooner had Totaro spoken these words than the Samebito uttered a strange wild cry of pain, and began to weep bitterly. And as he wept, great tears of blood streamed from his green eyes and rolled down his black cheeks and dripped upon the floor. And, falling, they were blood; but, having fallen, they became hard and bright and beautiful, became jewels of inestimable price, rubies splendid as crimson fire. For when men of the sea weep, their tears become precious stones.

Then Totaro, beholding this marvel, was so amazed and overjoyed that his strength returned to him. He sprang from his bed, and began to pick up and to count the tears of the Shark-Man, crying out the while: "My sickness is cured! I shall live! I shall live!"

Therewith, the Shark-Man, greatly astonished, ceased to weep, and asked Totaro to explain this wonderful cure; and Totaro told him about the young person seen at Miidera, and about the extraordinary marriage-gift demanded by her family. "As I felt sure," added Totaro, "that I should never be able to get ten thousand jewels, I supposed that my suit would be hopeless. Then I became very unhappy, and at last fell sick. But now, because of your generous weeping, I have many precious stones; and I think that I shall be able to marry that girl. Only – there are not yet quite enough stones; and I beg that you will be good enough to weep a little more, so as to make up the full number required."

But at this request the Samebito shook his head, and answered in a tone of surprise and of reproach:

"Do you think that I am like a harlot, able to weep whenever I wish? Oh, no! Harlots shed tears in order to deceive men; but creatures of the sea cannot weep without feeling real sorrow. I wept for you because of the true grief that I felt in my heart at the thought that you were going to die. But now I cannot weep for you, because you have told me that your sickness is cured."

"Then what am I to do?" plaintively asked Totaro. "Unless I can get ten thousand jewels, I cannot marry the girl!"

The Samebito remained for a little while silent, as if thinking. Then he said:

"Listen! Today I cannot possibly weep any more. But tomorrow let us go together to the Long Bridge of Seta, taking with us some wine and some fish. We can rest for a time on the bridge; and while we are drinking the wine and eating the fish, I shall gaze in the direction of the Dragon-Palace, and try, by thinking of the happy days that I spent there, to make myself feel homesick – so that I can weep."

Totaro joyfully assented.

Next morning the two, taking plenty of wine and fish with them, went to the Seta bridge, and rested there, and feasted. After having drunk a great deal of wine, the Samebito began to gaze in the direction of the Dragon-Kingdom, and to think about the past. And gradually, under the softening influence of the wine, the memory of happier days filled his heart with sorrow, and the pain of homesickness came upon him, so that he could weep profusely. And the great red tears that he shed fell upon the bridge in a shower of rubies; and Totaro gathered them as they fell, and put them into a casket, and counted them until he had counted the full number of ten thousand. Then he uttered a shout of joy.

Almost in the same moment, from far away over the lake, a delightful sound of music was heard; and there appeared in the offing, slowly rising from the waters, like some fabric of cloud, a palace of the colour of the setting sun.

At once the Samebito sprang upon the parapet of the bridge, and looked, and laughed for joy. Then, turning to Totaro, he said:

"There must have been a general amnesty proclaimed in the Dragon-Realm; the Kings are calling me. So now I must bid you farewell. I am happy to have had one chance of befriending you in return for your goodness to me."

With these words he leaped from the bridge; and no man ever saw him again. But Totaro presented the casket of red jewels to the parents of Tamana, and so obtained her in marriage.

NOTES

1. *Ryugu* is also the name given to the whole of that fairy-realm beneath the sea which figures in so many Japanese legends.

THE GOBLIN-SPIDER

In very ancient books it is said that there used to be many goblin-spiders in Japan.

Some folks declare there are still some goblin-spiders. During the daytime they look just like common spiders; but very late at night, when everybody is asleep, and there is no sound, they become very, very big, and do awful things. Goblin-spiders are supposed also to have the magical power of taking human shape, so as to deceive people. And there is a famous Japanese story about such a spider.

There was once, in some lonely part of the country, a haunted temple. No one could live in the building because of the goblins that had taken possession of it. Many brave *samurai* went to that place at various times for the purpose of killing the goblins. But they were never heard of again after they had entered the temple.

At last one who was famous for his courage and his prudence, went to the temple to watch during the night. And he said to those who accompanied him there: "If in the morning I am still alive, I shall drum upon the drum of the temple." Then he was left alone, to watch by the light of a lamp.

As the night advanced he crouched down under the altar, which supported a dusty image of Buddha. He saw nothing strange and heard no sound till after midnight. Then there came a goblin, having but half a body and one eye, and said: *"Hitokusai!"* ["There is the smell of a man".] But the *samurai* did not move. The goblin went away.

Then there came a priest and played upon a *samisen* so wonderfully that the *samurai* felt sure it was not the playing of a man. So he leaped up with his sword drawn. The priest, seeing him, burst out laughing, and said: "So you thought I was a goblin? Oh no! I am only the priest of this temple; but I have to play to keep off the goblins. Does not this *samisen* sound well? Please play a little."

And he offered the instrument to the *samurai* who grasped it very cautiously with his left hand. But instantly the *samisen* changed into a monstrous spider web, and the priest into a goblin and the warrior found himself caught fast in the web by the left hand. He struggled bravely, and struck at the spider with his sword, and wounded it; but he soon became entangled still more in the net, and could not move.

However, the wounded spider crawled away, and the sun rose, in a little while the people came and found the *samurai* in the horrible web, and freed him. They saw tracks of blood upon the floor, and followed the tracks out of the temple to a hole in the deserted garden. Out of the hole issued a frightful sound of groaning. They found the wounded goblin in the hole, and killed it.